Treasures
in the
Dust

TRACEY PORTER

Treasures *in the* Dust

JOANNA COTLER BOOKS
AN IMPRINT OF HARPERCOLLINS*PUBLISHERS*

Treasures in the Dust

Copyright © 1997 by Tracey Porter

For information address HarperCollins Children's Books, a division of
HarperCollins Publishers, 10 East 53rd Street, New York, NY 10022.

http://www.harperchildrens.com

Library of Congress Cataloging-in-Publication Data
Porter, Tracey
   Treasures in the dust / Tracey Porter
     p.   cm.
   "Joanna Cotler Books"
   Summary: Eleven-year-old Annie and her friend Violet tell of the hardships
endured by their families when dust storms, drought, and the Great
Depression hit rural Oklahoma.
   ISBN 0-06-027563-4
   [1. Depressions—1929—Fiction.   2. Dust storms—Fiction.
3. Oklahoma—Fiction.]   I. Title.
PZ7.P83395Tr   1997   96-54860
[Fic]—dc21   CIP
                                                                     AC

Typography by Al Cetta
1 2 3 4 5 6 7 8 9 10
❖
First Edition

Reprinted by arrangement with HarperCollins Publishers.

ACKNOWLEDGMENTS

Many thanks are due to the following:

to my mother Susan, my father and stepmother Bruce and Linda, and my stepfather Larry— All my life I have felt loved, and this more than anything has given me the confidence to write

to Francesca Lia Block, girlfriend, girl goddess and guide, who generously gave advice, counsel, and opened doors

to Jeannie, dancer, yogini, oldest friend, and good witch, who read all my false starts, every draft, and offered wise and loving words every step of the way

to Annetta Kapon for the year she opened her home to me and provided me with a room of my own, and to Sarah Torgov for also making me feel I could stumble into her guest room, laptop in hand, to write for a few hours

to Crossroads School for granting me a yearlong sabbatical and allowing me to fulfill a lifelong goal

to the Society of Children's Book Writers and Illustrators for awarding me a work-in-progress grant, giving me both confidence in my writing and money to pay the baby-sitter

to my friends in Cimarron County, Oklahoma: my hosts Ray and Gloria Damron; my tour guides Richard and Rita Scheller; and the three ladies who shared their brave stories of living through the Dust Bowl—Thelma Tevebaugh, Lyda Moore, and Ruby Barnes

to my teachers— From my elementary school teachers at St. Pius X who nurtured in me a love of the written word and told me I was a writer to my current teacher, zen-daddy poet Peter Levitt, I have been blessed with excellent teachers. I would also like to thank my college writing teacher, poet Roland Flint; wise-woman Lisa Victor; yogi Erich Schiffman; and my very loved and missed Max Junior

and finally, to my husband, Sandy, who tag-team parented with me during the hard revision, who always gave me love, made me laugh, and helped still the storms

for Sandy
because he broke the spell

for Sarah and Sam
that they might have the gift of friendship

Chapter One
Annie

Mama says the first storm came the day I learned to walk. I've heard the story so many times I know it by heart. I was fixed on her apron, fussing to be picked up while she kneaded dough. Something outside took my interest, and as if I had known how all along, I let go. Before I could fall down the stairs, Mama scooped me up in her arms. She danced me across the porch when a strange sight stopped her.

Our yard was full of a mismatched flock of birds. Mourning doves and sparrows, black-birds and starlings circled themselves and squawked. Some were nervous and agitated. Others were so weak they dragged their wings on the dry, hard earth that was once our vegetable garden. Off in the distance, a black cloud rolled over the land. Big as a mountain, it looked like it could cover all of Cimarron County. Lightning scattered the birds across the sky. Holding me tightly against her chest, Mama ran to the field calling for Pa.

For the rest of the day and through the night, my family huddled together under the kitchen table. Pa turned it into a tent by hanging blankets over it and weighting them down with jars of Mama's canned fruit. Mama held me under her apron to keep the dust out of my lungs. My big brother, Liam, says the wind was so strong the dust sounded like sand rattling against the windows.

That was the first storm my family faced. By the time I was talking, we had struggled through dozens. Dust is as much a part of my life as sunlight and air. Sometimes it is invisible, mostly it is silent, but it is always with us. It drifts through our house like a ghost, partially filling a teacup left out on the counter, smudging the tops of picture frames and the blue willow platter hanging on the wall. It scrapes the key when Pa winds the clock. It seeps through cracks in the windows and fills the grooves in the floorboards. We hear it grinding into the wood when we walk. It covers my pillow when I sleep. In the morning the only white space is where I've laid my head. Days after a storm, the ceiling sags with the weight of the dust collecting in the attic. Pa shovels it out through the ventilation window, and it becomes a waterfall of dust.

Mama says the look of the land makes her heartsick. Maybe because it's all I've ever known of home, I think it is pretty here. Dunes shift and change every day. They curve around the barn like arms and change a fence clogged with tumbleweeds into a dinosaur spine.

Sometimes the winds expose Indian campgrounds that time buried long ago. After a storm I go out searching for arrowheads. I keep a shoe box of treasures hidden under my bed. There are spearheads carved from flint, and tiny arrowheads no longer than my thumbnail carved from obsidian. I look at them at night before I turn down the lamp, imagining what life was like when the Plains Indians lived here, and there was nothing but prairie grass and buffalo as far as the eye could see.

When Mama looks sad, I climb into her lap and hold her. She worries that a spell of hard times is surrounding my childhood. She wants me to know what it's like to play hide-and-seek in a cornfield. She wants to see me skipping through a spring shower, mouth open, drinking drops of rain. Sometimes she worries we'll have to move west and work the fields like so many other families in our county, but Pa says this won't happen to us.

The old rocking chair creaks on the porch. Cicadas rustle their wings. I want to tell her what the storms have taught me. I want to tell her how I want to be an archaeologist and travel the world digging for the past. But she seems too sad for me to talk of when I will leave the family. My name is Annie May Weightman. I am eleven, watching the sunset from my mother's lap.

Chapter Two
Violet

When Aunt Miracle came to live with us, all she brought was a bag of clothes and a walking stick. Her tired old body looked like a question mark leaning on that stick as Pa led her through the house describing rooms and furniture. She's been blind for years, but until the dust settled in her lungs she was able to look after herself just fine. She lived all alone in a cabin near Black Mesa. Then the doctor told her she had to come live with us.

I was helping Ma put her things in the bureau when she told me to come sit down by her on the settee. She ran her fingers over my face and said, "No, your nose and cheekbones ain't like mine. Mouth ain't either." She squeezed my wrists, felt my hands, and pushed a thumb in the hollow of my palms. Ma was over in the corner frowning at us, her hands on her hips.

"The likeness ain't in our hands, either, but

Violet, there's something about you that's like me. I ain't figger'd it out yet, but it'll come to me." Aunt Miracle's cloudy eyes stared into space. She was rocking her body in that way blind people have.

"Go on, now Violet," Ma said. "Go start the washin' while I finish unpackin' for Aunt Miracle."

Outside by the barn, Ma told me how Aunt Miracle's rocking is a habit she's taken on, not one that comes natural.

"Only people born blind rock back and forth like that! It's so like Miracle to put on airs, pretendin' she's somethin' she's not." We were wringing out the laundry and hanging it to dry.

What's wrong with pretending? I asked myself. *Seems like I spend the better part of a day talking story to myself.* My family's clothes hung in the still air like sad flags.

One night before Aunt Miracle moved in, I heard Ma and Pa talking in the kitchen. Seemed like they were having a disagreement.

"She'll make more work than she can help with," I heard Ma say. "We're barely able to keep the kids fed and clothed as it is. I don't see how we can take on another burden."

"Miracle ain't a burden, Nevvie. She's family. Ain't never been a time when the Cobbles ain't taken care of their old folks."

"I know, Arthur. I know what you're sayin' is right. I'm just scairt 'bout survivin', 'bout feedin' and clothin' everyone. Seems like we're gonna have to move west sooner or later, but what with Miracle and the baby, I don't see how we can do that."

I couldn't tell for sure, but it sounded like Ma was crying. Outside the wind howled. I huddled in my blankets, turned my face to the wall, and pretended to be asleep. Once they left the kitchen, I whispered to my family of corncob dolls.

"Don't you worry none. This here family's gonna survive. Ain't nothin' gonna make us leave our home." I bent the father's wire arm a little tighter so his little hay fork wouldn't fall. I turned back to the wall again and tried to sleep.

My family's been hard hit by drought and dust. One duster killed all our chickens and all but one of our cows. Used to be we could trade eggs and butter and cream for credit at the general store. But now, we're lucky if Miniver produces enough for us to trade for our weekly loaves of bread. This hurts Pa. Before the drought our farm was known clear up to Elkhart for our sweet-tasting butter and cream. It shames him to get beans and potatoes on relief.

I'm the only one old enough to help out around the house. The twins are only four years old, big enough to need food and clothes, but too little to help Pa mend fences or milk Miniver. Every day baby Joseph needs more watching. He's starting to pull himself up and trying to walk. It used to be that Ma could carry him around in a bureau drawer while she saw to things. Now she's saying she might need me to stay home from school to help watch him. I try not to think about that. I like school. I don't want to stop learning.

A week or so after she moved in, Aunt Miracle figured out how we're alike. We were kneading the dough I had just made, and I was telling her how determined I was to get the dust taste out of our bread. I can't figure out where it's coming from. I keep the flour in three bags, double-sift it, and store the yeast in a Mason jar.

"It drives me crazy! We could all be pretending we're eating at a banquet back in fairy-tale times, but that taste won't let us! It just has to remind us that we're here in Cimarron County, Oklahoma, smack in the middle of the worst drought ever known."

"Why, aren't you a sensitive thing, Miss Violet," Aunt Miracle chuckled at me.

"Yes, I am," I answered back. "I am sensitive. Sensitive and delicate like that girl who felt a pea under a pile of mattresses and was crowned a princess. And I am going to work this dust taste out of our bread. Tastes like when I was little and put my tongue on the screen door."

"Well!" Aunt Miracle slapped the table. "I know what it is now. You're what I call a mind-full girl. Your mind is full of stories. Me, too. Been that way all my life."

What she said caught me unaware, like a bell ringing out of nowhere. I stared into her poor dull eyes, and before I could stop myself, I told her the one secret I have in the world.

"I still play with dolls. Even Annie don't know I do." I stopped talking, trying to come up with a reason why I told her. "I hope I don't wake you up since we're sharing the front room." Our tiny house only has one bedroom. My parents sleep there with the baby. The twins sleep on the floor on a mattress Pa sawed in half. I sleep on the other half in the front room. Aunt Miracle sleeps on the settee.

"That won't bother me, child. What kinda dolls do you have?"

I got my three corncob dolls and placed them in her hands.

"Why, aren't you clever! You made them arms out of wire so you can pose them!"

"Yes, ma'am," I answered. "I made the mother's bonnet from a scrap of burlap and the baby's blanket from a flour sack." Aunt Miracle took a long time feeling all the different fabrics and the shape of the clothes.

"This is a sweet doll family, Violet. You go on playin' with them. I won't tell nobody at all."

Ever since that day, there's been a bond between us. Aunt Miracle is the only grown-up who makes me proud of my imagination. Mostly, it gets me scolded—scolded for daydreaming at school and for not doing my chores fast enough. Only Annie and Aunt Miracle like me being as mind-full as I am.

Before Aunt Miracle came, I used to wonder if that dust taste was coming from me. After all, I told her, I've grown up with dust storms and drought. Maybe the dust has worked its taste into my skin and bones.

We were settled into bed, but we were still talking about this and that. "Maybe my skin ain't never touched enough water to taste normal," I added.

"Now here's a time when your mind is workin' too hard. You put your mouth on your hands and tell me what it tastes like."

"Tastes like nothing. Tastes like skin," I said.

"That's what I thought you'd say." Aunt Miracle laughed softly in the dark. "Only dust in you, Violet, is fairy dust."

Chapter Three
Annie

I'm a plain brown bird of a girl. A sparrow. I can blend in with the dust if I want to. My hair is brown, my eyes are brown, and my arms and legs are bony and long.

My best friend Violet is more like a hawk. Her hair is reddish gold, and her eyes are fast and bright. She moves swift and proud, darting in and out of moods lightning fast. She wants to be an actress and is always getting me to help her act out a fairy tale or a book. I usually play the woodsman or the prince while she plays the wicked stepmother or the princess who's been bewitched. If my heart's in a story, I might argue with her for the good part. But most of the time I like watching Violet more than I like playacting. She wears her hair long and arranges it differently for each role she plays—pigtails for Little Red Riding Hood, on top of her head for a queen. I have Mama cut my hair short. Archaeologists don't have time to worry about their hairstyle when they're digging up an ancient temple.

On Sundays after church I go home with Violet. We take turns reading to her blind aunt. Because she has three little brothers as well as Miracle to help with, Violet has a lot more work at home than I do. But of all Violet's chores, reading to Aunt Miracle is her favorite. Like Aunt Miracle, Violet is story crazy. She can carry her baby brother on one hip, fix oatmeal for the twins, and tell them the story of Cinderella at the same time. Sometimes I think that if Violet didn't have so many chores, she wouldn't have such an imagination. Either it had to grow fierce or die, and since it didn't die, it's as strong as the storms that ravage our farms. We can be looking for a lost button in the schoolyard, and Violet is following a treasure map, looking for a chest of gold. Sometimes it gets irritating, because it's hard to tell where or who Violet is. She's airy, always looking to fly away. I'm happiest sitting on the ground, digging for the past.

It is late Sunday afternoon. I am waiting for a hailstorm to pass before I walk home. The hail is the size of gumdrops. It falls white to the ground, then pops up covered in dust. The twins are building a tower out of empty spools and matchboxes. Violet's parents and Aunt Miracle are listening to the radio. The baby is asleep in Mrs. Cobble's arms. We're passing the time wondering how our teacher, Miss Littlewood, is spending the summer.

"I bet she's off in England studying all those kings and queens she told us about," says Violet. "She was partial to that king with the six wives."

She has a far-off, dreamy look on her face. Her hair falls over one side of her face. She loops it over an ear, watching the storm intently. In my mind, I recall Miss Littlewood is visiting her parents in Amarillo, but since that would spoil our game, I keep it to myself. Miss Littlewood is young and pretty, the only woman we know who wears lipstick. It is easy to imagine her on some kind of adventure. She's been our teacher since we started first grade at Garlington School.

"I bet she's on a safari in Africa so she can teach us all about lions and giraffes. I bet she falls in love with a big-game hunter and never comes back."

"Oh, no!" exclaims Violet. "That would be terrible! Did she really go on a safari?"

"I just made that up," I assure her. "Actually, I think she's probably in Amarillo visiting her folks." To Violet, this is almost as bad as if she ran off and got married, never to return. She gathers her legs to herself and rests her chin on her knees.

"I guess that sounds more likely," she replies glumly.

When the hail stops, Violet walks me to the gate. The hailstones look like scattered marbles. We roll and teeter on them, pretending we're on roller skates. The sky is a watercolor of gray and blue. The windmill makes lazy turns in the now soft wind.

"I bet Miss Littlewood comes back with all kinds of new books for us to read," Violet yells after me.

"I bet she does, too-ooo-ooo," I yell back. My voice fills the empty road, bouncing off the pavement. Off toward Black Mesa sun pours through a break in the clouds.

Chapter Four
Violet

Ma's been telling me to act more responsible and get to my chores without her having to holler at me. There are things I got to do now that Annie's gone home, but instead I climb up the windmill. Used to be I was so afraid up here I couldn't stand up. I walked around the narrow walkway on my knees, afraid either I'd get dizzy if I stood up or the wheel would knock me over the railing.

Nowadays our windmill isn't good for nothing but the view. It pumped up all the water long ago. Pa says he's gonna tear it down and use it for firewood before the boys figure out they can climb it. He doesn't know I come up here. Mostly I come to be alone. Sometimes I pretend I'm the first mate of a pirate's ship looking for a ship to attack. Lately I've been thinking about how things might be in California if we end up moving there. Folks say it's the land of milk and honey. Maybe we'll have a white house. Maybe I can learn to tap-dance like Shirley Temple. Off in the distance I can make out Annie walking home along the road. She's a dark little figure, about the size of one of my dolls.

In the kitchen, I sort through the beans soaking in the big green bowl, throwing out the hard, wrinkled ones and the little rocks. I rinse them again, then pour them in the soup pot with a ham hock and a chopped onion. I used to like cooking. When Ma first started teaching me, it made me feel grown up. Lately it's beginning to feel like any other chore, something I have to do, not something I like doing. If I don't go to school, my days will be filled with nothing but chores. I haven't told Annie yet that I might not be joining her come September.

If I do have to stay home, Aunt Miracle says she'll keep me company while I take care of the baby and do the chores. She has lots of stories to tell. Most of her adventures came about because of a snakebite.

When Aunt Miracle was a baby, a rattler bit her left hand. It made her whole arm swell and sent her to sleep. The preacher, the Cherokee healing woman, and the doctor all came to help. No one could wake her, and everyone thought she would die. Three days later, on her first birthday, she woke up. She was strong and healthy as before, but the little finger on her left hand never grew up with the rest of her. It stayed exactly the same size as when the snake bit her. Even today, ninety years later, Aunt Miracle's finger is smooth and pink as a baby's.

Her parents took her recovery as a sign from God and changed her name from Sue to Miracle. Folks came from miles around to see her and her tiny finger. She appeared in medicine shows and carnivals from San Antonio to Santa Fe.

"I'm beholden to that snake," she said after she let me take a good long look at her strange, waxy finger. "It kept me in shoes during my childhood and gave me the chance to see some of the world."

Mostly she tells me her stories at night before we fall asleep. But if she feels strong enough, she'll sit with me in the kitchen while I'm working. "Did I ever tell you how my pa and I traveled with a caravan of gypsies through the Sangre de Cristo Mountains into Colorado?"

She's found her way into the kitchen to keep me company while I make the bean soup for supper.

"Why, no, you never have, Aunt Miracle."

"Oh, those gypsy ladies were purty! They wore gold coins in their hair and flowered skirts. They danced barefoot around the campfire while their menfolk played violins. Most folks were scairt of them. Said they're baby snatchers and thieves. But they was good to me and Pa. Helped us find the pass through the rough part of the mountains. Somewhere I still have the copper pot they traded us for Pa's hat. Now I wonder . . ."

Before she can finish, a coughing spell interrupts her story. I dash around the table and slap her between her shoulders. Most of the old folks in these parts suffer like this. Dust has settled deep in their lungs and makes them cough and wheeze. Sometimes a fever takes hold and infects their lungs. The doctor calls this dust pneumonia. It's what everyone fears when old folks and babies get sick after a storm.

Bent over double, Aunt Miracle coughs and coughs into a handkerchief. Her face is red with straining. Pa runs in from the front room to help, but by the time he gets here, the coughing has stopped.

"Thank you. Thank you, both." Her voice is a faint whisper.

"Hush now, Miracle. Let me help you back to your bed," says Pa. He slips his arm around her and guides her to the settee.

Later on, I bring her a bowl of soup and a thick slice of buttered bread.

"Here, eat this."

I hold the spoon up to her mouth and she takes little sips. Sometimes it's hard to figure out what Aunt Miracle needs help with. She gets insulted if one of us tries to do too much for her. On the other hand, she's too proud to ask for help when she really needs it. Tonight, I can tell by the way her hands are shaking that she needs me to feed her.

"This is good, Violet," she says. "I think you're beginning to get rid of that dust taste."

By the time I finish the dishes and crawl into bed, Aunt Miracle is asleep. I'm worried by her recent coughing spell. She'll need an extra-exciting book to keep her in bed. Before falling asleep I try to remember some of the books Miss Littlewood has by her desk. It seems to me there was one she was always trying to get me to read about an Arabian princess who told such fantastic stories it saved her life.

Chapter Five
Annie

The day after the hailstorm, a dust cloud rolled in from the north and covered the county. Two days later Violet and I are standing on a hill of dirt, sunk to our ankles. Even though dust no longer falls from the sky, our mothers insist we wear bandannas across our faces. Violet has been reading the tales from the *Arabian Nights*. She says we look like Arabian princesses.

"Come, Princess Sharma. Our camels await to take us to Baghdad!" With that, Violet runs down the hill, kicking up a cloud of dust as tall as she is.

As usual, when we are playing one of the games she has made up, I am running behind her, trying to keep up. Her imagination is far bigger than mine, bigger than the emptiness that surrounds us. For her the dust storms have turned Cimarron County into the Sahara Desert. Where I see abandoned farms and half-buried tractors ruined by dust, she sees camel trains and oasis after oasis circled by palm trees.

Violet's golden-red hair is the only bright color in the landscape. Both our dresses are faded and patched. Our tired brown shoes are scuffed. If it rains enough to grow wheat, our mothers tell us, they will sew us matching dresses. We want yellow dresses with white flowers.

"Perhaps we should have a white satin sash," I suggest after I catch up to her.

"Don't talk about that!" Violet snaps. Above her bandanna, her blue eyes flash with anger. "We're playing Arabian princesses."

"Forgive me, Princess Fatima. Let's ring for the slave to bring us more figs."

"Oh, stop it. The game is ruined now." Playing make-believe with Violet is like being in a different world with its own rules. The most important rule is not to interrupt the story with things that have to do with our daily lives. She says it disturbs her concentration.

We trudge on, stopping at a soapweed the size of a soup pot. I put on my gloves to hold the needles back while Violet cuts it off at the root. We're gathering weeds and cactus leaves for our cows. Only one man in the county feeds his livestock properly. A fork of the North Canadian River runs through his land and he can grow feed corn. The rest of us make do with whatever we can get our cows to eat—soapweed, prickly pear, and Russian thistle, mostly. My family's been luckier than Violet's. Since we have a full coop of chickens as well as five milk cows, we can trade eggs and cream for feed every now and then. Pa says even a little bit of feed keeps them healthier than most of the other cows in Cimarron. But Violet's family has only one cow, and they lost their chickens in a dust storm. They're barely able to trade for the food they need for the family, let alone for feed for Miniver. They need every weed and cactus Violet can find to keep that skinny cow producing.

"Why don't you take the whole thing," I suggest as Violet starts to cut it in half.

"No. We're working together so we share everything we find." She stuffs the soapweed into the burlap bag trailing behind her. It's an old cotton sack, one her daddy used as a boy when he picked cotton in Texas.

"Let's get some leaves off that prickly pear over yonder," I say and the two of us run off. A trail of dust hangs in the air behind us.

We walk home dragging our sacks on the ground so the cactus needles and soapweed spines don't prick our backs. Our faces are flushed and sweaty because of the bandannas. We remove them while we sit on the trunk of an uprooted cottonwood tree to empty our shoes. Something dark and glassy glints in the blazing sun. I reach for it quickly, knowing what it is even before I touch it.

"Hey," I say. "Look at this arrowhead." I hold it up for Violet to admire. It is almost as long as my hand, much larger than the others I've found. Carved from black obsidian with a perfect point, it is a prize find, one my big brother Liam will envy.

"I bet it's a Comanche," I add. "I bet it's for buffalo hunting." The name Comanche makes my heart beat faster. Pa says they were the best horsemen in the entire Southwest.

Violet dutifully inspects my prize. "Very nice," she says, but I can tell she is not impressed. She couldn't care less about the tomahawks, bones, or arrowheads the dust storms uncover. She has given me most of the things she has found, including a spear point.

"Why, you don't even think this is interesting, do you? Do you know how old this is? Do you know that the man who carved this edge didn't have proper tools? Do you know he probably hammered it out with just another rock?" I'm feeling angry as I talk. It seems to me that more and more the only things Violet cares about are her fairy tales and myths. "We don't have any of the same interests anymore," I go on. "I don't even know why we're best friends."

"Well, whatever made you think best friends have to be just the same?" Violet is angry, too. Her eyes are flashing. "Why would I want to be with someone exactly like me? I don't love fossils and arrowheads like you, but that don't bother me. I like it that we're different. I like learning from you, and I like getting you to play and do things you wouldn't normally do."

She's right, I think. In a way I'm learning from Violet and she is learning from me. How else would I have dressed up in an old sheet, pretending to be a Greek goddess, if not to act out one of the myths Violet fell in love with?

Violet smiles at me. Like a storm cloud, her anger has come and gone. She takes the arrowhead and looks at it carefully. "I bet you're right. I bet this is a Comanche arrowhead. I bet it belonged to the chief."

Violet and I resume the Arabian princess game on our way home. We chatter about camels and Ali Baba, peacocks and snake charmers. When we are near to where our mothers might see us, we tie the dreaded bandannas back on.

At home I dump my bag of cactus leaves and soapweed into the crate by the barn. It overflows with what I've gathered over the past few days. The dark of the cool barn draws me in. I laze there a while before heading out to the henhouse to gather eggs. The hog is sleepy in the heat. It grunts with curiosity, but doesn't bother to get up to see if I'm carrying a pail of slops. I lean against the ladder, lightly pushing the point of the arrowhead into the palm of my hand to feel its sharpness.

When night comes, I sit on a milking stool by the corral, watching Pa singe the spines off the cactus with a weed burner. Tongues of bright orange and yellow flame leap up. Pa uses a long poker to pull the cactus away before it burns too much. Flora and Bluebell moo and shift impatiently behind the fence.

It is the first clear night after the storm. Stars shine like pinpoints of light. The sweet-smelling smoke collects in one thin ribbon and climbs to the sky. Liam and I toss the cactus to the cows. They gobble them up greedily. When we're done, I pull my arrowhead out of my pocket and show Liam.

"Why that's a beauty, Annie May," he says, holding it by the firelight. "In fact, it's good enough to be mine!" I try to snatch it back, but he waves it over my head, taunting me. I slug him as hard as I can in the stomach, but he just laughs at me. I am almost breathless with anger. I fight hard to keep from crying in frustration.

"Pa! Pa!" I yell, finally giving in to calling for help. "Make Liam give me back my arrowhead." Liam mocks me under his breath. "Pa! Pa! Pa!" he whispers in a girlish voice.

"Now, Liam, give that back to your sister. You're too old to be teasing her like that."

"But, Pa, she's too young to appreciate this one. It's too good for her to take care of."

"Annie takes fine care of her collection and I'm sure she'll take good care of this one. Let's see what you got there, Miss May."

Proudly, I hand it over for Pa to inspect. He studies it carefully. "Why, this is a beauty. Looks like it was carved yesterday. Sharp, too."

"Can I go to town with you next week and show it to Mr. Coates?" Mr. Coates knows all about the Indians who lived here.

"You sure can. I bet he asks if he can put it in the library's display case. If he does, he'll put a little plaque under it that says 'from the collection of Miss Annie May Weightman.'"

Before I go to sleep I put my arrowhead under my pillow. All night I dream I am among Comanche warriors, braiding a long rope of horsehair into the manes of stallions. When our enemy attacks, we throw ourselves into the loop and slip under the bellies of our horses. Bullets and arrows sing past us. Laughing, we ride deep in the night to the safety of our campground.

Chapter Six
Violet

Pa sets his rifle down when he sees me opening the gate, dragging the burlap sack behind me. He takes the sack from me and opens it.

"Is this all you could find?" He looks disappointed. We're trying to feed Miniver as best we can since her calf is coming soon. We hope it's a heifer so we'll have more cream and butter to trade in town.

"Yes, Pa. Annie and I took all we saw and we walked clear over into old man Schiller's property."

"Don't let him see you. He's liable to set his dogs on you if does." Pa looks again into the half-empty sack, then slings it over his shoulder. "Keep your eyes open next time you're out walking."

I follow Pa into the barn. Hanging head down from a hook on a post are a pair of jackrabbits. Pa probably shot them this morning while I was out with Annie. Their eyes are wide open, and their hind legs are stretched as if they died just as they were leaping in the air.

For some reason, mice and rabbits are living and breeding and eating just fine in this drought. The mice are just plain pests, running between the walls in our house and getting into the sacks of beans and rice. The rabbits, on the other hand, are helpful. If it weren't for them, we wouldn't eat any meat at all. We gave up raising hogs long ago. They're too expensive to feed. Before that duster killed all our chickens, Ma traded eggs for beef at the general store. Ma says we're lucky to have the rabbits Pa kills.

Miniver lumbers over to get a better look at me and Pa chopping up the soapweed. She's slow and patient now that she's gotten so big. She bides her time waiting for us. She nuzzles away the dust on the surface of her water trough, then takes a long drink.

"Pa, do you think I could help you birth Miniver's calf?" It's a question I've been storing up for the right time. Girls don't usually get to help at a calving. It's a trade boys learn, so they can get a job as a ranch hand somewhere. I reckon that since Pa knows there's gonna be meat for supper, he'll be agreeable.

"Well, that's usually boy's work. But since none of the boys is old enough, I'll give it a thinking." As if to bear witness to what Pa has just said, the twins run through the barn, whooping and hollering, tumbling over each other like puppies.

"When do you think her calf will come?"

"I'd say in a couple of weeks. Just about the time you go back to school."

Even though I am afraid to hear his answer, I ask anyway.

"Do you think I'll be going back to school?"

"I hope so, Violet. We're doing all we can, but times are hard. We all have to make sacrifices." And as if he can't bear to face me, Pa picks up the rabbits and takes them out back to clean them. As he walks away I notice how the sole of his left shoe is torn away from the upper. It flaps as he walks, and I can see his bare heel.

Inside the house, Ma is churning butter. Baby Joseph is napping. Aunt Miracle is asleep too. She is propped up with pillows so she is almost sitting. Doc Barnes told us it would be easier for her to breathe that way.

"How's she doing, Ma?"

"She's been better. Her lungs are awful

congested. Thank heavens she's got no fever. It ain't the dust pneumonia yet."

"Did she get up this morning?"

"No, she's too weak. She was askin' for you before she fell asleep. Don't wake her, though. Sleep is the best thing for her. Take over the churnin' for me. My arms are tired."

I take her seat, turning the big wooden spoon of the butter churn. From the window, I can see Ma wiping her hands on her apron as she walks over to Pa. They're both frowning. Pa kneels to pick up a stick and writes something in the dirt. Ma bends down with him, studying. She looks over to our house, then up to the sky and shakes her head. Finally, he hands her the fresh-skinned rabbits and she walks back to the house, almost dragging the red, gutted bodies in the dust.

Chapter Seven
Annie

Mr. Coates, the librarian, leans back in his chair and runs an ink-stained fingertip across the blade of my arrowhead. His gray hair sticks out like short wings above his ears. Pa calls Mr. Coates an "eccentric." Mama says he feels more comfortable with books than with people. Folks tend to look after him because of his strange ways. They don't even bother to honk when he walks out in the middle of the street reading a book. They just stop and let him pass by.

A shaft of sunlight from the window above his desk casts a perfect square of light on the wooden floor. I hook my thumbs through the straps of my overalls and do my best to look serious as he inspects my arrowhead. While waiting I try to read the titles of the archaeology books on the wall behind his desk. There are shelves and shelves of books I want to read—*Riddles of Ancient Egypt*, *When Dinosaurs Roamed*, *Painted Caves of Early Man*. I want to learn how the Egyptians built their pyramids and made mummies. I want to go to Italy and dig up things that belonged to the Romans and see the caves that Cro-Magnon man painted in France.

Violet, who has come into town with me and Pa, is browsing through the library. She is looking for a mystery book to read to Aunt Miracle. I can see the blur of her pink dress as she skips to the next aisle.

Mr. Coates turns the arrowhead over in his hand. He closes one eye, then looks at it so closely that his nose nearly touches it.

"Well, Miss Weightman . . ." he begins in his deep voice, "this is a fine specimen, indeed. Look at how delicately the blade is carved. If the craftsman had used just the slightest bit more force, he would have broken it."

"Do you think it's a Comanche?" I ask.

Mr. Coates pulls out a handkerchief and slowly polishes his glasses. "Well, now, that's hard for me to say. It would be a rarity, of course. There was a time when the Comanche hunted bison from Nebraska all the way to Mexico. But they haven't lived here in the pan-handle for nearly two hundred years." He puts his glasses back on and folds his hands on his desk. "I am certainly no expert. However, my friend Professor Stevens at Edmond State College is. I'm planning on visiting him next month, and if you like, I'll take your arrowhead with me and ask him to take a look at it."

"I'd appreciate that, Mr. Coates. I sure want to know all I can about this one."

Mr. Coates takes out a piece of blank paper and a black-and-gold fountain pen from his desk drawer.

"Now, Annie, here's something you should learn. Whenever you hand over something of value, it is customary to receive a receipt."

Mr. Coates writes out a few lines then reads aloud to me,

"Received from:
Miss Annie May Weightman
One antique arrowhead

I am in possession of her arrowhead for the sole purpose of presenting it to Professor Andrew Stevens and asking him to identify its origin.

Mr. Robert L. Coates
Cimarron County Library
Boise City, Oklahoma"

I fold the piece of paper in quarters and put it in the pocket on the front of my overalls. I snap the pocket shut.

After Violet checks out her book, we walk down Main Street to the general store. Liam and Pa are buying sewing needles for Mama, new milk pails, barbed wire and eightpenny nails to repair the fence. The street seems sad today. Nearly every other store is closed down because so many people have left for a better life in California. A stack of faded posters for the Ringling Brothers circus is propped up against the window of one of the abandoned storefronts. I kick an old can. Violet balances her books on her head, walking with her arms outstretched like a tightrope walker.

"How do you reckon those fire-eaters in the circus swallow flames?" she asks. I know exactly where she is right now. She's not walking down Main Street of Boise City. She's wearing a sequined leotard, leading the parade through the big top of the circus. Playing circus used to be one of her favorite games when we were younger.

"I think it must be some kind of trick," I answer. "It just isn't possible for a human being to eat fire. Your stomach would burn up." We wave howdy to Miss Farrell, the waitress at Golden Grain Diner. She calls out for us to say hello to our folks. "We sure will," we holler back.

It takes my eyes a minute or two to adjust to the dark of the general store after the glaring sun. Liam is admiring a black leather saddle in the window. He ignores us as we come in. Pa is in the back, leaning on the counter, talking with the other farmers who have come in to do business. I hear him laugh softly with the others and say, "Well, you know, it rains at the end of a dry spell. Always has. Still, I just don't believe things in California are all that easy. Why, I was reading in the Amarillo paper just the other day how plenty of our people are doing field work for pennies. Even their kids are picking." Two milk pails shine by his boots like a new dime. He and Liam brought in an extra-big load of butter, cream, and eggs for trading. The men tip their hats to me and Violet and say howdy.

"How'd your visit with Mr. Coates go?" Pa asks.

"Bet he said it was just a common ol' Kiowa

arrowhead like everyone else finds," sneers Liam. But in spite of himself, he has edged up to me and Violet to hear my news.

"No, he didn't either," I answer. "He's taking it to his friend at Edmond College in Oklahoma City to look at. He gave me this." I unfold the paper and hand it over to Pa.

"Well, look at this." He reads the receipt aloud. One of the other men looks over his shoulder to read with him. "This here means he thinks it's special."

"He wouldn't bother to take it with him if he thought it was a Kiowa arrowhead, would he?" I ask Pa, sneaking a smirk at Liam.

"No, I don't believe he would." And then Pa surprises us by adding, "Let's get some soda pop for the ride home."

When we unlatch the door to the cooler, delicious, icy air escapes. It floats over my arms and face and covers my upper body like a scarf. Before I can make a memory of it, it disappears.

On the way home, Liam sulks in the back of the truck. Violet and I sit in the cab with Pa, savoring our orange sodas, trying to make them last all the way home. Our fingerprints melt into the frosty bottle. My orange pop is so cold it tastes like it was made with snow. Pa asks Violet if her cow has had its calf yet. Violet says no, then goes on to say how her Pa is going to let her help him birth it. The two-lane road stretches straight out in front of us. I think about the Kiowa and Comanche campgrounds that lie long-buried beneath the dry land. Secretly, I touch the note in my pocket to make sure it is still there.

Chapter Eight
Violet

At first Ma wasn't too pleased about me helping Pa birth Miniver's calf. Aunt Miracle's been
needing more and more care. Pa rigged up a little tent over her bed so we can treat her with
steam. All day long, a pot of water with herbs
and eucalyptus oil boils on the stove. Every
hour I put a fresh, steaming bowl of the medicine on the floor next to her. It helps loosen her
cough and soothe her throat.

"I might be needing you the day the calf
comes. What if Aunt Miracle is having one of
her spells? What if the dust pneumonia sets in?
I've only got two hands. I can't do everything by
myself."

I have no answer for her. I pull one of my
pigtails around and begin to rebraid it.

"Well." She softens. "Miniver's a good birther.
You probably won't be out of the house that long
anyway. All right then, you can help your Pa.
Long as I don't need you for something special."

When the day finally comes, Pa is out in the ruined orchard chopping down trees for firewood. I run out to fetch him. My feet kick up so much dust, I'm choking.

"Pa! Pa!" I have to stop and cough before giving him the news. He is knee-deep in withered branches. "Miniver's water broke, just like you said it would. She's all still and quiet-like, looking at me with big eyes."

"Those are the signs, Violet. I'll be there shortly."

"Ain't you comin' now, Pa?"

"No. I want to finish chopping this tree. There's plenty of time yet. You go sit with her. Talk to her every now and then, but not so much to make her nervous."

I run back to the barn, following the same cloud of dust I kicked up moments ago. I can hear Pa's ax echoing behind me.

It's sunset when Pa comes into the dark barn. He hangs an oil lamp from one of the rafters, then spreads some clean hay around bulging Miniver. He whispers to her. She's barely moved since her water broke hours ago. As Pa places his hands on her huge belly, she stares at me with sorrowful eyes.

"Shouldn't something be happening by now, Pa?"

"Not necessarily," he says. "Go fetch me some soap and a bowl of hot water."

Pa washes and dries his face and hands. He puts one hand deep into Miniver's backside to check on the calf. He flinches a bit, as if a rock sailed by, barely missing him. There isn't too much that can go wrong in the birth of a calf. If it's in right position, hooves first followed by the head, it's a simple affair. But Pa's expression tells me something's not right.

"The calf's turned backwards. It's a big calf, too. Nothing to worry about yet, but it's gonna be a hard labor for Miniver." Pa washes his bloody hand and takes off his shirt. "Go cut a piece of rope about six feet long and make a loop in it."

When I hand it to him, he says, "Now listen careful. Here's what we're gonna do. I'm gonna slip this loop around the calf's jaw. Once I say so, I want you to start pulling slow and steady on the other end. Don't jerk it now. And don't use all your strength either. Just slow and steady."

With each of Miniver's contractions, Pa's

hand is squeezed right against her pelvic bones. I hold the rope, watching Pa's face, anticipating when he'll give me word to start pulling. Finally, I see an expression of relief on Pa's face. He's snared the calf's jaw.

"Start pulling, Violet. Don't use too much force. Between contractions I'm gonna try to push the calf around headfirst."

The oil lamp casts a smoky, golden glow in the barn. The only sound is Pa's short little groans as he pushes the hind end of the calf. It seems like hours of this go by. We are both exhausted.

"The calf's dying. It's too big and it's suffocating," he says out loud, talking not to me or anyone but to God and the universe. His white back is heaving as he rests his hands on his knees, trying to catch his breath. His arm is covered in blood. His face and chest are splattered.

Finally he says, "Come on, Violet, let's try again. Pull harder, now. Use all your might."

I pull with every bit of strength I have in me. The rope burns my hands. I face the other way and loop it over my shoulder so I can get more traction. Finally, there is a sickening give that sends me stumbling over my feet. The calf is half born. Its hooves are bent back, the most dangerous position for the mother. The dead calf looks out to the world with still, glassy eyes. Its gray, swollen tongue hangs from its mouth.

"Oh, lord," Pa cries. "This is all wrong. I've got to try to save Miniver. Git out of here, Violet. Go in the house. Don't come back out."

I run to the house, tears streaming down my dusty face. My mother meets me at the door and picks me up like I was little again.

"Minnie's dying, Ma. Minnie and her calf are dead."

Chapter Nine
Annie

I walk my fingers along the wire Pa tied from the windmill to the henhouse. It's only mid-morning, but already the wire is warm from the sun. Pa put the wire up as a guide so he can check on the chickens in a storm. Some storms are so dark, it's impossible to find your way in your own backyard. If the chickens aren't in the coop they can blow away in the winds. Violet's family lost all their chickens this way last spring. The winds were so fierce and the sky so black, her pa couldn't find his way to shoo the chickens into the coop. The next day as he drove into town, he saw dozens and dozens of small humps in the road. Turned out those humps were all their chickens. The storm blew them over a mile away and covered them with dust.

Some of the hens peck my hands when I take their eggs. Today I replace one or two of each hen's eggs with an egg made of chalk.

They don't fool the chickens, but they help keep the snakes away. If a snake eats a chalk egg, it'll die since it can't digest it. It's been a bad summer for bull snakes. I've seen one that swallowed three eggs at a time coiled around the fence post closest to the barn. That's how a snake manages to break the eggs inside. Sometimes you can hear the shell cracking.

It's a bright, cloudless day. Sun bounces off the white eggs in my basket. Inside the kitchen, Mama is measuring a cup of raisins, something I haven't seen her do in a long time.

"What are you baking with those raisins?" I ask. For nearly a year the only thing Mama has had to sweeten a dessert has been corn syrup. The sight of Mama baking with raisins is almost as exciting as a bag of threepenny candy. It is the first week of August. I quickly run my mind through the month and can recall no birthdays, no holidays.

"I'm making bread pudding for you to take over to Violet's family," she answers. She adds the raisins to a bowl of bread crusts soaking in eggs and milk, then sprinkles in a teaspoon of cinnamon.

"Why?" I ask. The air in the kitchen is

heavy and still, even hotter than outside because the oven is going. Mama stops to dab her forehead with a corner of her apron.

"Seems that Aunt Miracle has taken a turn for the worse. She's stopped eating and won't get out of bed. I thought maybe my bread pudding could tempt her."

"Why doesn't Violet's ma make bread pudding for her?" I ask. I sneak my fingers into the bowl and pick out a raisin.

"Get your paws out of there, Annie May!" She mockingly hits my hand with her wooden spoon. In a more serious voice she says, "You should know they're having a hard go of it over there. They've had worse luck than we've had, and they've got seven mouths to feed. Lord knows how they've managed."

My mother's words strike me strange. Everyone in the county is facing hard times, all us kids know that. Yet, it never occurred to me that Violet's family is worse off than us. To be honest, I've always kind of envied Violet. She seems more important than I do. My chores save my mother time and trouble, but Violet's keep her family going. She's as necessary as either of her parents. Not many Cimarron girls get to help their fathers birth a calf. And, of course, it wasn't anyone's fault that both the cow and her calf died. Pa said it was a difficult birth. Not even the best ranch hand in the county could have saved them.

Mama smoothes the top of the pudding with the back of her spoon then sits down on the stool to face me.

"I've been meaning to talk to you since that cow and her calf died. I think you've got to start preparing yourself in case Violet and her family head west. They've been hanging on for the sake of Aunt Miracle, and when she dies, seems likely to me that they'll be off to California. They've got no milk cow anymore. No cream or butter to trade for food and clothes, and no money to buy 'em with." She reaches over and picks a downy chicken feather from my hair. Sunlight streaming through the window gives the eggs I gathered a halo.

"Why can't we give them some of our eggs? Why can't we share some of the ham in the smokehouse and some of our butter and flour?"

"Honey, we've been doing that, and we'll go on doing so as long as they stay. But Arthur and

Nevvie have four children to raise, four to clothe and feed and send to school if they can. As it is, Violet has to stay home from school to help keep things going. So, before too long, I think, they'll head out for California. They're probably figuring that's the best place to give the family a chance to live a decent life."

"But why?" I ask, suddenly frightened that my mother could be right and that Violet might be leaving me soon. "Why would they go now? If they want to go to California why didn't they go before?"

"Well, honey, I think they've been wanting to leave for a while, but Aunt Miracle couldn't survive the journey. They say there's a terrible desert folks have to cross. A great rocky, barren stretch of land without any sort of shelter. I've heard some Cimarron families had to bury their old folks in a pauper's grave alongside the highway in that awful place."

"Aunt Miracle's not dying, Mama. She's a strong old lady. She's just feeling poorly. Your bread pudding's gonna pick her up."

"I hope you're right, Annie May." Worry collects in two deep lines between her eyebrows. It's a look I've come to know in my mother. "I just don't want you to be too upset if Violet has to leave."

Later that day, after supper, Liam and I walk over to Violet's house. He carries two jars of canned tomatoes and lima beans and some ham in a paper bag, and I carry the pan of bread pudding. In the dust on the road are drop craters from a minute-long rain that fell around noon.

"Ain't even a public rain," Pa said, looking out from the barn. Still, he held his hat up to catch some drops and let some fall on his head. He sighed when it was over and went back to fixing the loose boards of the hog pen.

For the first time I can remember, the fields look lonely to me, and I wonder if the moon could be a drier, sadder place than our county.

"I'd quit your worrying, Annie May," says Liam. "Aunt Miracle's got a quarter Cherokee blood in her, and that snakebite made her tough."

"You think so?" I ask.

"Heck, yeah," Liam answers. "Who else you know survived a rattler bite as a baby? They say if it doesn't kill you, it makes your heart awful strong. Gives it an extra lifetime or two, sort of like a cat."

Once we pass the line of willows by the dry creek bed, I can see Violet's house. She's there on the porch walking baby Joseph. Her folks come out to greet us while the twins keep busy chasing each other around the windmill and the privy. Violet's ma looks sort of faded, like a photograph left out in the sun.

"Hey," says Liam, as he hands Mrs. Cobble the bag of food. "You folks see any rain at midday?"

"Is that what that was?" chuckles Mr. Cobble. "Been too long and lasted too short for me to know for sure." He and my big brother wander over to the barn, talking. Mrs. Cobble tells me to make sure I thank my mother and carries the bread pudding into the kitchen. I take the baby from Violet and play "this little piggy" with his toes.

"You remember that Shirley Temple movie we saw in Kenton?" Violet asks. She stares at her feet, watching them make circles on the dusty porch with her toes.

"Sure do," I answer. "It was called *Little Miss Broadway*, and Shirley tapped up a storm."

"Well, I've been thinking that I sure would like to take some tap dancing lessons. Seems to me I'd take to it pretty easily." She practices some shuffling steps and little jumps. Her skirt tosses around her brown legs like a bell.

"I think you would be good at it," I reply. "Too bad there's no dancing studios around here."

"Yes, it is too bad. Ain't nowhere to learn ballet or tap here. Bet there's all kinds of dancing schools in California. Bet there's a dancing school on every block out there in Hollywood."

Violet pirouettes back and forth across the porch, arms outstretched. She hangs on to the post and lets gravity pull her in a slow, sweeping arc to her knees. Baby Joseph starts to whimper and fuss. When I can't soothe him, Violet stops dancing and takes him from my arms.

Chapter Ten
Violet

Mostly I minister to Aunt Miracle alone. Ma says just the sound of my voice might help her get well. There are days she doesn't even know I'm with her, but I go on reading anyway. I finished the tales from the *Arabian Nights*. Now I'm reading *The Jungle Book* to her.

Aunt Miracle's face is empty and gray. My corncob dolls have more life than she does. She lies still. Her hands curl into tight little claws and grip the sheet. Only her tiny finger, pink and unwrinkled, seems alive. The only time she moves is when she coughs so strong it jerks her body off the pillow.

When Annie visits, we take turns reading and making her comfortable. We keep a cool, damp cloth on her forehead and draw the curtains to keep her room cool. Annie starts a new chapter of *The Jungle Book* while I warn off the flies buzzing around her face.

My mind drifts as Annie reads. Tomorrow is

the first day of school, but I won't be going. In the summer, I was hoping Annie and I could show up on the first day both wearing yellow dresses. In my mind I saw us showing off in front of the other girls, and me whispering to Annie during class and getting her in trouble with Miss Littlewood. But until Aunt Miracle gets better, I'll be staying home to help Ma.

And if she doesn't get better, and if she dies, Ma says we'll head off for California. Lots of families from these parts have already gone west. Folks say there's plenty of work and no one goes hungry. There are fields and orchards everywhere, and you can just take what you need from the side of the road. With all the scrambling Ma and Pa do just to keep beans on the table, I guess this sounds good. But mostly what I think about is getting to Hollywood and taking dancing and singing lessons. I bet there are shops and shops full of sparkly tap shoes and fluffy dresses. I keep these thoughts to myself, 'cause I know Ma and Pa are counting on me working the fields with them. I've been learning about keeping dreams in a little box inside you. Sometimes it just isn't right to bring them out into the light.

"Just think, Violet," Ma says, pulling me close one night before I creep into bed. "After a few months of field work, we can settle down, maybe even buy a piece of land. We can get you back in school."

"But I don't wanna go to school in California. I want to go to Garlington School with Annie. I want Miss Littlewood to be my teacher."

"I know you do, child. But there ain't no future here. We're just barely feeding the family, and if things get any worse, we won't even be able to buy cornmeal. And the bank will take our farm away 'cause we can't pay back the loan we took out last year. At least in California, we have a chance to live right. We'll be able to eat and dress right, and we'll send money back to pay off the bank and keep our farm. This land's been in your daddy's family ever since the Oklahoma Land Rush. His grandpa built this place. It'd break him to lose the land he was raised on."

I hear Ma and Pa talk into the night about heading out for California. Their voices drift through the cracks in the wall. They float above Aunt Miracle's wheezing like a scarf in a breeze. For the first time in ages, Ma sounds young.

After they've gone off to bed, I lean my dolls against the wall. Their faces are worn away with dryness and dust. I stare at them, trying to conjure what they looked like when Annie and I first made them. Once they had smiles. They used to whisper stories. They'd tell me about fairies dancing in the briar patch wearing thimbleberries as hats. I keep listening for their voices, wondering if they know what will happen to me.

The sound of Aunt Miracle's wheezy breathing fills our room. She's working hard for each breath. If only it would rain. Water would heal her lungs and make it so we could stay home.

Chapter Eleven

Annie

I'm tired when I get home from Violet's house, more tired in my mind than in my body. For the first time I can remember, I go to bed early before the first day of school. Starting sixth grade just doesn't have any excitement for me since Violet won't be there. She won't be waiting for me by the seesaw in the morning or getting me in trouble with her whispering. I feel lonely just thinking about walking through the door of Garlington School. Even the thought of seeing Miss Littlewood doesn't raise my spirits. Before climbing into bed, I scrub my face and hands extra hard, as if I could wash the sadness away from me.

In bed, I turn the lantern low. I look through my box of treasures to choose one to put under my pillow. There are rocks and bones, the receipt Mr. Coates gave me, a turtle shell, a snake skin and sixteen arrowheads. The two smallest ones were probably carved by the same person. I found them right next to each other the day after a big dust storm. They are root-beer colored, carved from obsidian. When we studied geology last year, Miss Littlewood said obsidian is Mother Nature's glass. It was formed millions of years ago when volcanoes dotted the land and fired up the sand so hot it turned into glass. They're cool in my hand, with delicately chipped edges and sharp points. There's a knifeblade lashed to a broken shaft and the chipped tomahawk Violet gave me. I think about the long arrowhead carved of black obsidian that Mr. Coates is researching for me. Is it really a Comanche? I wonder. I try to remember if there are any milky patches or if the obsidian is pure black. Try as I might, I can't picture it in my mind exactly. I cup each stone in my hand to feel its impression in my palm. As if putting it under my pillow is a kind of prayer for her and Aunt Miracle, I choose the spear point Violet gave to me.

This school day, my first day in the sixth grade, begins like any other. Mama makes oatmeal with cinnamon sugar and bits of dried apple. She serves it with cream. As she returns to her bread baking, I can feel her watching me and Liam out of the corner of her eye, making sure we eat it.

"Well, looky here," says Pa as he walks in the kitchen. "Looks like two smart school kids to me."

As he has on the first school day of every year, Pa has prettied up our shoes. We may not have new shoes to wear on the first day, but Pa has polished our hand-me-downs to look good as new.

Since the road is clear of the drifts and dunes the federal government pays him to clear, Pa allows us to ride Wisecrack to school. We're the only family for miles around that still has a horse. Horses have a terrible time in these dust bowl times since their lungs are so sensitive. Five or six times a day Liam has to wipe the dust from Wisecrack's nose. It's one of his chores.

"Take him slow, Liam," directs Pa as he gives me a boost into the saddle in front of my brother. "Don't let him gallop, but if he starts to, make sure you hug your sister steady with your legs. And you, Miss May, don't let go of the saddle horn." It's a speech we know by heart, one we've heard probably every day that we've ridden Wisecrack to school.

About halfway to school, Liam brings Wisecrack to a stop and jumps off the saddle.

"Well, Annie, he's all yours."

"What do you mean?" I ask.

"It occurred to me last night. I was in the sixth grade when Pa finally allowed me to ride Wisecrack to school. So I think it's time you started riding him part of the way. Today I'll even let you ride him into the schoolyard."

Speechless with pleasure, I slide back into the saddle as Liam draws the stirrups up to fit me. Wisecrack drops his great white head and shakes the flies away from his eyes. When I'm all set and ready, Liam walks alongside us as Wisecrack and I take a slow, clip-clopping pace.

"Does Pa know?" I ask finally.

"Nope. Let's just keep this between ourselves. With things like this, it's best if we can find a way to let him think it's his idea."

It isn't the first time I've ridden Wisecrack all by myself, but it's my longest ride and the first time I've taken him to school. Liam is true to his word, letting me show off a bit in front of the other kids by riding him to the gate and tying him up in the little corral.

I am disappointed when, as she passes out books, Miss Littlewood hands me a sixth-grade reader.

"Miss Littlewood, ma'am, I finished this last year," I remind her. Her first-day-of-school outfit is happy as Christmas. She is wearing a red-and-white checked dress, a black-velvet bow in her hair, and black shoes.

"I'm sorry, Annie, but the seventh- and eighth-grade readers haven't arrived yet. In the meantime, I'd like you to help some of the others in the class begin this reader. Rita Barnes, Burris Amble, and Thelma Schiller are all rather behind in their reading skills. I'd like to make the four of you a little reading class unto yourselves with you as the teacher."

At first I feel a flush of pride. Rita, Burris, and Thelma, however, are not so pleased with Miss Littlewood's proposal. When I turn in my chair to smile at them, they glare back.

On the playground at lunch, Thelma makes her feelings on the matter clear to me. After walloping one of the older boys at tetherball, she stomps up to me as I'm eating my sandwich.

"Don't you think for a moment that you can put on airs with me, Annie May Weightman!" Her face is red as she shakes her finger at me. "I may not know my letters good as you, but I can lick you and your brother any day of the week." Then, as a final show of her toughness, she wipes the sweat off her face with her arm, turns her head to the side, and spits like a boy. She stomps across the playground, her hands in fists.

The rest of the day, thankfully, is boring and uneventful. I enjoy the handwriting lesson most of all. Now that I am a sixth grader, I get to write with an ink pen. At the beginning of the year, Miss Lightwood gave me a wooden pen shaft with three brass nibs of different sizes. The smallest nib is so sharp it tears your paper if you press too hard. The medium one is the easiest to work with, but my favorite is the largest. It's a tiny circle, about the size of a pinhead, and collects a lot of ink for big, sweeping lines. I take a long time dipping the nib into the little fat-bellied pot of blue ink. I practice my cursive capital letters in my fanciest handwriting, including lots of loops and trills wherever I can fit them in. The E's, F's,

T's and P's are especially fun.

On the ride home, Liam reminds me that the Schillers are mean old folks.

"Just plain snake-vicious if you cross 'em. Pa says old man Schiller shot someone dead for drawing water from his well. He's never gotten over the fact that some people got their land free during the Oklahoma Land Rush, and he's passed that bitterness on to his family. My advice to you is that you treat ole Thelma as if she was smart as Thomas Jefferson. Ain't no one like to be talked down to, least of all a Schiller."

"You think she might all of a sudden haul off and hit me?"

Liam considers this a moment then shakes his head. "No. I don't believe she would. Long as you treat her fair and respectful, I think Thelma will do the same."

At home, Mama has cornbread and fresh buttermilk for us. She sits down with us as we eat our snack, a rare thing, for daylight is precious and shorter autumn days mean she has less time to finish the laundry. She fiddles with the clothespins in her apron pocket as we talk. Outside the sheets on the clothesline billow and snap in the gusty wind.

"So you're gonna help Miss Littlewood teach reading. How 'bout that," she says with pride.

"She better watch her step with Thelma Schiller," Liam interjects. He crumbles his cornbread into his glass of buttermilk then drinks it. It's a habit he's picked up from Pa.

"I think that's good advice," says Mama nodding her head.

"I do, too. I intend to follow it," I answer. There's a pause in the conversation, one of those sudden quiet moments that some folks say means an angel is flying by.

"Violet was over here this morning," says Mama.

"Oh?" I'm surprised.

"Yes, I'm afraid she came with some bad news. . . ."

And before another second passes, I know what Mama is going to say next.

"Aunt Miracle died last night. She passed away peaceful. The doctor says her heart just stopped beating."

Chapter Twelve
Violet

For once there's nothing for me to do. No chores to finish and no babies to look after. Neighbor ladies have come to cook and watch the little ones while we go to the funeral. Annie and I are left to ourselves. We wander around listening to the women talk about how big the twins are now or how well my ma is holding up or how peaceful Aunt Miracle's passing was.

"I've got an idea!" says Annie. "Let's watch our ma's fix Aunt Miracle's body. I've been reading all about how the Egyptians bury their dead. Let's see how us Cimarron folks do it."

"Okay," I reply weakly. I can't say I really want to do this, but I'm too numb to be contrary.

We creep over to the window and peer into to the kitchen. Aunt Miracle lies on an old quilt covering the big oak table. Mrs. Weightman lights a candle and places it above her head. Ma ties up her jaw with a strip of cloth. Then she holds Aunt Miracle's eyelids down and places a silver half-dollar on each closed eye. It feels like a dream even though I can see and hear everything plain as day.

"I feel badly we can't give her a church funeral," Ma says. "She always liked a purty funeral."

"Now don't you worry 'bout that, Nevvie," says Mrs. Weightman. "This is going to be a fine burial. She's surrounded by family and friends, and the preacher's coming to say a few words. When it's my time, I'd be happy to be dressed and buried by family and neighbors. It's better than having paid folks at your side."

Ma lets out a long sigh. "I s'pose you're right. Just seems like things aren't the way they're s'posed to be. Seems like things are just too hard."

And then our mothers fold the quilt about Aunt Miracle's legs and shoulders. One by one Mrs. Weightman hands Ma big safety pins. Ma pins the quilt neatly around the body.

"She looks kinda like a mummy," Annie whispers to me. It's true, I think. She doesn't look like my aunt. But at the same time, it seems a disrespectful thing to say.

"You go on watching," I whisper. "I'll wait for you by the woodpile."

When Annie joins me, we head out to the front yard to meet her father. Wisecrack is leading their big hauling wagon up the yard to our barn. Mr. Weightman ties him to the windmill. He removes his hat before entering the house. A few moments later, he and Pa carry Aunt Miracle's bound body out of the house and lift it into the wagon. Her eyes shine silver in the last bit of daylight.

It's the magic time of day. For a few minutes, anything catching a slant of sunlight looks like it could burst into flames. All of a sudden, I'm filled with a longing to run away. I don't know how I'm going to face watching the men lower Aunt Miracle into the earth and then, maybe only a week from now, saying good-bye to Annie and leaving home. My windmill looks fragile and despairing against the sunset, like a ship being swallowed up by an angry sea.

"C'mon, Violet," Ma calls me. I pile in the front seat next to Annie. The neighbor ladies bring the twins and baby Joseph up to touch the coffin and say good-bye to Aunt Miracle. Pa and some of the other men ride in the back. As we head off for the graveyard, Annie puts her arm around me. I don't have anything to say. I keep my hands folded in my lap.

At the grave, the preacher says a few words about Aunt Miracle, how God saved her life when she was a baby and how she paid Him back by being kind and truthful all her life. When the prayers are done, Ma, Pa, and I each throw a handful of dirt into the grave. The neighbor men stay to finish the burying. Mr. Weightman takes us back home. The night is thick and black. A barn owl swoops over us then disappears into the dark.

"I miss you at school, Violet," says Annie. I know she means well by saying this, but I feel too far away to say something back. The only sound is Wisecrack's hollow steps on the road. I turn away as if I'm looking at something on the other side of the road. I don't know why I can't talk to her. Maybe I'm preparing her for when I'm gone. Maybe I'm too tight with sadness to say anything.

As I let my face fall against my mother's side, I overhear Annie whisper to her mother.

"That's the strangest funeral I've ever been to. Nobody cried."

"Shh-hh, Annie," Mrs. Weightman whispers back. "There's lots of ways to show sorrow."

Hearing this, I realize it's a strange sort of sorrow I'm feeling right now. It's the sorrow of Aunt Miracle's passing mixed with the sorrow of knowing soon we'll be leaving everything we know. Already, I am far away from Annie. My family and I are in a separate world now, lost somewhere between staying and leaving.

Chapter Thirteen
Annie

Pa says that part of the sadness of the folks who leave Cimarron is that when they leave this land, they leave part of themselves. This is the land their kin has worked for generations. They've been here through flood years and dust years. They tilled and plowed and planted and harvested cotton, corn, mustard, and wheat. Their folks lived and died here. This is where they thought they'd see their grandbabies born and themselves buried. Even if California really is the land of milk and honey, we can never be truly at home there. This red, dusty land is us.

It wasn't more than a week after Aunt Miracle was buried that the Cobbles sorted through their things preparing to go west. They had a little sale at their house, selling some things and giving away others. Pa gave Mr. Cobble five dollars for a horse collar, a hand plow, and a box of tools. Mrs. Cobble gave Mama her bread board and her flour bin. Violet and I played on her porch while our parents and the other neighbors negotiated and traded. We were quiet mostly, drawing hopscotch squares with a broken chalk egg. Finally it was Violet who spoke.

She didn't look up at me. She stared at the ground, writing numbers in all the squares with the worn-down piece of chalk.

"As soon as we get some kind of address, will you write me? I'll be sending you postcards and letters from all over California, telling you about my dancing lessons and my new school. I sure would 'preciate hearing back from you."

"Of course," I answer quickly, wondering what exactly Violet is feeling right now. Sometimes she seems happy to be going so near to Hollywood where she can take singing and dancing lessons, and maybe become a star like Shirley Temple. Other times, like today, she seems so tired and weary she can't feel much of anything.

On the way home, Mama holds Pa's arm, and they talk between themselves. I trail behind them, pretending to be looking for hawks resting on the fence posts, but really I'm trying to listen in. They're talking about the Cobbles going to California. I hear Mama's worried voice saying things like "sounds too good to be true," and "no schools in those migrant camps." Pa doesn't say much. He never does when Mama gets to worrying. Mostly he just listens. He pats her hand every now and then, but I do hear him say something like, "Arthur Cobble needs his dignity. He's got to try to hold on to his land and give his family a better life."

Folks like us who haven't left hear all kinds of stories about California. Mostly they're pretty stories, stories about endless fields and orchards just waiting to be picked. Sometimes a neighbor will show Pa a handbill talking about how much work there is and how high the wages are. For a while Liam was all fired up about us leaving. I remember how excited he was the first time a neighbor showed Pa a handbill calling for a thousand pickers to work the fruit orchards in California. We were out in the barn, cutting open new bales of straw and spreading it on the floor.

"Picking grapes and oranges and peaches sounds like nice work, Pa. Even if they wouldn't let you eat some, I bet you could snitch a little ol' ratty peach every now and then. Seems to me you wouldn't ever go hungry if you worked in the fields. Besides, I ain't tasted grapes since I was six years old."

I understood this argument of Liam's. All us Cimarron kids are taste crazy. Between the drought and the Depression, there aren't many good things to eat. I've heard of more kinds of fruits than I have actually tasted. Mama does the best she can by putting dried apples and occasionally raisins in bread pudding, but I'm longing to taste peaches and grapes.

"Just remember one thing, Liam," said Pa. "Few things in life are as good as people make them out to be. All those handbills claiming high wages and lots of work are just selling people a pretty story. Of all the folks who've left Oklahoma, I ain't heard any of 'em's gotten rich. Mostly what I hear is about living in tents and trucks, moving from place to place looking for work, kids picking crops in the sun instead of being in school, old people working—it sounds pretty miserable to me. A writer fella wrote an article for one of the big San Francisco newspapers about how terrible things are for our people out there. A man I met at the general store in Elkhart showed it to me the last time

I was up there delivering butter."

"Then why are folks leavin', Pa? If things are so bad there why are they leaving home?" I asked.

"Because folks are desperate, Annie. Families like the Cobbles have it awfully tough. Their land is mostly sandy to begin with, and the drought and the storms have ruined what land there was good for planting. They don't have nearly enough money to invest in milk cows or chickens. And he's got his bank loans to worry about as well as providing for his family. Maybe he'll make enough money out there to pay off his loans and come back once the rains return. I know that's what he's hoping for. He doesn't want to stay away forever. Some folks leave Cimarron saying they never want to set foot here again. But not Arthur. He's tied to this land. He's as much a part of it as Black Mesa."

I think about this conversation as we walk home, turning it over in my mind, realizing it should have been one of my first clues that Violet and her family would have to leave.

Days later, my family and I come to say good-bye to the Cobbles. It's early morning, and they're hoping to light out before noon. Violet's standing in her front doorway, halfway in the house, halfway out, twirling a lock of her hair. Her pa is boarding up the windows, hoping that the glass will still be there if and when they ever come back from California. The back of their rusty old Model-T is packed high and covered with a big tarpaulin. All the hauling and packing has kicked up the dust. A new film of it rests on the headlights and the hood. It floats and dances through streams of early morning sun.

Liam is excited. He helps Pa and Mr. Cobble fasten the tarpaulin over the huge pile of clothes and food and kitchen things stacked on top of the mattresses.

"Your pa letting you ride in back of the truck?" he asks Violet.

"I got to," she answers glumly. "There ain't no room for me in the cab. The twins and the baby and Ma are riding up there with Pa."

"You're gonna have the best view." Liam nods his head with enthusiasm. "I sure wish I could see that desert folks talk about. Those mountains, too. You're lucky. I'd wanna sit back here."

Even though I know this day's been coming, it's still hard for me to believe that Violet is actually leaving and that I may never see her again. I find it hard knowing what to say to her. I've already repeated my promise to write. I search my mind for something else to say.

"Hey," I say after a time, surprised I have a genuine question for her. "You bringing along any mementos?"

"I'm bringing these." She reaches into the pocket of her dress and pulls out three old corncob dolls.

"I remember these," I say as she hands them to me. "We were playing with these before we were in school."

"Yeah, well, maybe I can keep one or two in the pocket of my overalls when I'm working. They'll remind me of home." For a second or two, Violet looks me right in the eye as if she might say something else. Then she drops her gaze to the ground.

For the umpteenth time, Liam checks the straps of the tarp making sure they're secure. Mr. Cobble lifts the hood and watches the engine run. Pa walks up to the front porch and takes off his hat.

"I've come to say good-bye, Miss Violet." He shakes her hand. "I think your parents are mighty lucky to have a strong, helpful girl like you. You be good and mind them. Help your mama. Annie, why don't you come with me to say good-bye to Mrs. Cobble."

"Pa, can't we stay and watch them go?"

"They've got an hour or two more work to do. Besides, leaving home is a private thing for a family. Come on."

Inside, Mama is holding Baby Joseph and whispering with Mrs. Cobble. The house is empty and strange, dark from the boarded-up windows and more quiet than I've ever known it. A stack of cut sandwiches sits on a piece of brown paper, ready to be wrapped up for the road.

"I've come to say good-bye, Nevvie," Pa says. It's the first time I've heard him use Mrs. Cobble's first name. "I'll come by every now and then to check on the place, make sure it doesn't fall to ruin before you come back."

"You and Ida have been mighty good neighbors." She reaches out to take Pa's hand. "If we meet folks half as kind as you along the way I'll count ourselves lucky. You be a good girl, Annie

May. You keep studying and learning. I hope to get my girl back in school soon."

"Things are gonna be all right, Nevvie. Either things get easier for you folks right away, or you get yourselves back home to Oklahoma."

When I say good-bye to Violet, my heart feels cold and heavy. Her head is dropped and her golden-red curls hide her face. I pick up her lifeless hand and lace my fingers through hers. She doesn't look at me or say a word.

"'Bye, Violet," I say. "Be sure to write, ya hear?"

As my family finishes our good-byes, the wind picks up. Little tornadoes of dust, dust devils some call them, whirl by the windmill and the teetering, overpacked Model-T. Folks say they're reminders. Two months or more might pass between dust storms. You can get tricked into thinking the storms are over and better times are on their way. But then the wind blows and those dust devils start twirling, reminding you how dry the earth is, how much rain is needed before things can be right again.

Chapter Fourteen
Violet

Octobertime, 1938
near Holbrook, Arizona

Dear Annie,

We've been driving Route 66 ever since we hit Amarillo. Oklahoma folks call it the Mother Road because so many of us are traveling it, searching for a better life. It's a long road. Pa says it would take us past Hollywood and straight to the Pacific Ocean if we followed it to the end.

As we headed near Albuquerque we saw the prettiest mountains you could imagine, sort of like the hills around Black Mesa, but wilder and more vast. Layers of blue and purple mountains pile up against the horizon, and just above them are layers of pink clouds. The map says these are the Sangre de Cristo Mountains, the same ones Aunt Miracle crossed when she and her Pa were in medicine shows showing off her tiny finger and telling the story of her snakebite.

Somewhere, miles beyond, are fields for us to work. When the weather's fine, I perch up on the pile of mattresses and watch everything we pass. Sometimes I think about what we've left behind. Sometimes I think about California, dreaming about the white house we'll live in and the dancing and acting lessons I'll take.

Pa says it might be a month or more before we get to the San Joaquin Valley. That's where all the field work is. We've got to take it slow or else our car might not make it. We'd be in a right sorry state if this old Model-T breaks down so bad Pa can't fix it. It rattles and shakes going up any kind of steep hill. It's already broken down twice. The first time Pa packed an axle bearing with a pork rind. The second time he had to hitch into town to find work so he could fix it proper. We camped with some other folks near a bridge on the banks of a little creek while we waited for him. He was gone for three days. When he came back he had the parts he needed to repair the axle, plus some ham hocks and beans, and a few extra dollars. He got work unloading box cars at a train depot and hauling lumber into a lumber yard.

The folks we camped with have been on the

road longer than we have. They've been in these parts for quite a spell picking cotton and lettuce, and now they're heading farther west again. They've been zigzagging back and forth between California and Arizona chasing the crops. They say there isn't no proper campsites until we cross the Mojave, a big old, angry desert. They're all from Oklahoma too, over near Beaver. We're the only family that's still holding on to a farm back home. Everyone else lost their land when the bank foreclosed on it or the farmer they were sharecropping for knocked down their house and forced them to leave.

At night Ma and Pa sit with them by the campfire telling stories. Hearing them makes me understand why Ma and Pa packed us all up so soon after Aunt Miracle passed. Sooner or later we'd be exactly where we are now. Only now we're better off, 'cause we still have a chance to keep our land. The other night I overheard Pa tell Ma the last thing he did before hitching back from the depot was send a few dollars to the bank holding the deed.

I've seen lots of folks with proper tents to sleep in. Pa didn't want to spend the money on one. He says we got to save all we can for the lean times.

I told him I thought these were the lean times, but Pa says no, long as we've got food and a little money, they aren't lean. So we do the best we can with the old blankets and tarps we brought from home. We camp between trees so we can string them up on the branches. Then we pin them together down along the sides to make our little shelter. Last thing we do is haul the mattresses down from the top of the truck and set them under the blankets. Every morning Ma and I wash clothes in the little stream and hang them to dry on the cords holding up our tent. I bathe baby Joseph in a tin tub. Sometimes when I see him in that oval tub by the water I remember the Bible story about baby Moses being rescued by the Pharaoh's daughter. I look at my brothers playing by the creek and wonder if some rich lady might pass by in a fine car and take pity on us. Maybe she would give us one of her rings or a necklace so we could sell it and go back home.

Ended up we camped near that creek for five days. When we first got here we were too tired to eat. We were so worn out from traveling and set-ting up camp we slept in our clothes. Our meals have been pretty plain since leaving home—cold biscuits and beans, mostly. The ham hocks Pa brought back that one day made us feel like we were feasting.

Everybody we meet on the road is hoping to find the same thing we are—work picking cotton, peas, or fruit or whatever else is in season. Ma says she don't mind working in orchards, but she'd hate to see us kids work cotton fields. She picked cotton when she was a little girl in Texas. She says it's rough work, hard on your back and your hands.

I would have written sooner but paper and pencil are hard to come by. A waitress gave me this one I'm writing with. We were at a truck stop filling the car up and Pa gave me three cents to buy some penny candy for the twins and myself. He was feeling good about that extra money he made and finally getting back on the road to find work. The twins picked out what they wanted, but I told the waitress that what I really wanted was a pen so I could write my best friend. Ended up she gave me her own pencil and told me to pick out my candy, too. She was a nice lady. Pretty, too, like Miss Littlewood.

At first Pa didn't want to give me this hand-bill I'm writing on the back of. Turn this letter over, and you'll see it's calling for 800 pea pickers in Delano, California. But one day he got talking with some of the men at the gas station. All of them had seen the very same handbill and said it wasn't worth a darn. They said the ranch was already crowded with folks begging for work and that by the time we got to Delano the work would be gone anyway. One of the men took a whole pile of handbills pinned up to the bulletin board in the station and told Pa to go ahead and give them to me for my letter writing. He said they might as well be good to somebody for something.

So I guess we're heading off someplace besides Delano. I hope we get work picking fruit. I want to see what a great big field of trees looks like. I'm thinking it's cool and shady under the branches.

Say hi to your folks for me. I don't know when I'm gonna be able to afford a stamp and an envelope. I'll keep this letter folded up in my pocket until then. Things get lost easy when you're living out of a car, moving, unpacking, and packing back up all over again.

Love from your friend,
Violet Cobble

Chapter Fifteen
Annie

The other day I realized that besides the little reading group I'm teaching at school, Violet is the only person I've ever shared books with. We must have read and reread, playacted, and made up new chapters for *The Adventures of King Arthur and the Knights of the Round Table* hundreds of times. Even when we started looking in different shelves of the library because I was getting more and more interested in history and archaeology, I could usually get her interested in what I was reading. All I had to do was read her a description of a temple in ancient Rome and how the vestal virgins kept a fire going in front of a statue tall as a windmill. Her eyes would turn dreamy and soft and she'd hound me with questions once I finished. "What kind of clothes did these girls wear?" she'd ask. "How old were they and what did their parents say when they left to go work in the temple? Did they get to do everything in the temple? Where'd they eat and sleep, for instance?" She thought being a vestal virgin sounded like a real nice job.

"Get a book on ancient Rome and read it yourself," I told her. I guess it annoyed me that I couldn't answer all her questions. I like fancying myself an expert on ancient history.

"No, that's all right," she said waving her hand like I was some pesky fly. "I don't have time to get all interested in that now. These days I got to keep my reading time for stories. When Aunt Miracle is better and baby Joseph is old enough to play with the twins, I'll branch out to reading about true things."

Rita and Burris, on the other hand, are slow, tired readers, bored as afternoon dogs. I do the best I can to make the stories in their reader interesting. I tell them the plot before we start reading, trying to imagine how Violet would do so with her flair for drama. I change my voice for the different characters and gesticulate with my hands. By the time we start reading, though, they get a dazed expression, sort of like how Bluebell does when I milk her. Once Rita fell asleep. She almost toppled over in her chair before jerking herself awake.

For the most part they're pleasant enough. They don't hold it against me that Miss Littlewood has assigned me to help them with their reading, and I don't think they would be trying any harder if they were working with her instead of me. Somewhere along the line, they've just given up on school. Learning doesn't fit in with their lives or their dreams. Cimarron County is full of people like Burris and Rita. They don't want to travel or solve mysteries or read or write. It's a wild, rough land here in the panhandle, and it takes a different kind of smarts from school smarts to get by. They both have that kind of intelligence. You can see it in the way Burris rides his family's horse to school and Rita catches the snakes that hide under the schoolhouse. I admire the kind of smarts they have, but mostly being around the three of them just makes me miss Violet more.

Thelma seems to admire the kind of smarts I have, too, and she has surprised me with her effort. She listens hard when I prepare my little class for the story, scrunching up her forehead and biting her lower lip. She moves her lips as she reads silently, pointing to each word with a dirty finger and leaving a smudge mark on the page. She gets impatient when she comes across a word she can't decipher.

"What's this word? What's this word?" she asks, almost shouting, poking me in my upper arm. During the rest of the school day, she acts as if I don't exist. I take this as a compliment, knowing that if she didn't like me or didn't think I was helping her, she'd just as soon bully me on the playground.

It's a dreary November day. Halloween has come and gone. We made masks out of paper bags, dunked for apples at school and had black and red licorice whips at recess. There's a chill in the air, and the coat rack in the back of the room is full of raggedy coats and hats. All of us wear hand-me-downs from a sibling, a cousin, or a church sale, the same source for our shoes. My coat used to be Liam's. It's dark gray with suede patches on the elbows. One or two kids have to wear a grown-up coat that's been taken in here and there. I feel sorry for these kids. It's one thing never to have anything new, but it's another to wear something funny-looking because it's the only thing you have to keep warm.

Miss Littlewood, on the other hand, is looking bright and crisp as usual this morning. Her coat has a rabbit-fur collar and it hangs on a hook behind her desk. She's teaching us how to write a letter. Liam looks like he's daydreaming. It's a look I notice in him more and more when Miss Littlewood is teaching something at the board.

"Now up here, in the upper-right-hand corner," she says using the black-tipped pointer as she refers to a letter she's written on the blackboard, "is where you write your address. Then you skip a line and write the date. Then you skip two more lines, go to the left-hand margin and write the address of the person to whom you are writing."

She goes on to explain the difference between business and personal letters and the variety of polite closings one can choose for either one. Then she assigns us to write a letter ourselves. "I have stamps and envelopes for those of you who want to send your letter," she says as we begin writing.

At first I think of writing Mr. Coates to ask him what he's found out about my arrowhead and if I can get it back next time I go to town with Pa. Then it occurs to me to write Violet. I stare out the window at the bleak gray day, remembering the last time I saw her, how she was drawing on her porch with a bit a chalk, her hair hanging over her face. She's been gone two months, and I haven't heard from her. I don't know where she is, let alone how she and her family are getting along. I can't seem to get started on either letter. I'm frustrated and restless, squirming in my seat, tapping my pen on my desk, until Miss Littlewood calls me.

"Annie Weightman, why are you so fidgety? What seems to be the problem?"

"I can't decide who to write to. I have a business letter and personal letter I could write."

"Which one do you want to write?"

"I want to write the personal letter. Trouble is, I don't have an address, and I can't get it until my friend writes me."

"Is this friend Violet Cobble?" she asks. Just hearing Miss Littlewood say her name fills me with sadness. If I have to say much more, I might break into tears.

"Yes, ma'am," I answer in almost a whisper.

Miss Littlewood takes a deep breath before going on.

"I think you should write your letter to Violet. I'll save it here in my desk with a stamp and an envelope, and when you get her address, we'll mail it."

Back at my desk, I begin my letter. The rest of my group is nearly done with the assignment, but Miss Littlewood allows me to eat my lunch at my desk and finish mine.

RR 23 Box 12
Boise City, Oklahoma

November 13, 1938

Dear Violet,

How are you? In school today Miss Littlewood assigned us to write a letter, so I am writing you. How are you and your family? How is California? Is it as pretty as everyone says?

In school we're learning about the Roman emperors in history now. Seems like no matter what country they rule or when they live, kings and queens are all crazy. Miss Littlewood told us about an emperor named Caligula who made his horse a senator.

Miss Littlewood has asked me to help teach reading to Burris Amble, Rita Barnes, and Thelma Schiller. I wish you were here to help me, since I'm not as much of a storyteller as you. It's hard to get them enthusiastic about anything having to do with books or letters. Thelma is doing the best. She's moving ahead in the sixth-grade reader, and she doesn't glare at me anymore. In her own way, she's even showing me that she likes me. I guess she is almost becoming a friend, but she could never take your place.

I think of you all the time. Sometimes on our way home from school, Liam and I walk over to your house just to make sure everything is OK. Last time we were there two wild cats crawled out from under the porch. They're a skittish pair of rascals. They seem to be doing just fine, probably eating all the mice they can find.

School seems empty without you. Do you miss Aunt Miracle? I do. It's been eight weeks since you've gone, and I miss you more than ever. I still haven't heard from you.

Love,
Annie

I read my letter over twice before folding it in thirds the way Miss Littlewood taught us. She puts it inside a blank, stamped envelope and tells me she'll keep it safe for me until I get Violet's address.

That evening, during supper, we listen to the radio, a rarity since Mama thinks it's rude to do so while eating. Late this afternoon when Pa was trading some eggs for groceries at the store in Boise City, the men were talking about a huge duster blowing in from Colorado. On the radio, the weatherman in Colorado say it's the biggest black cloud folks there had ever seen. We can barely hear his voice beneath the spitting and crackling static of our old radio:

"A pilot, blinded by the black blizzard, was forced to land his plane in a barren field. A housewife, lost in her cornfield, survived only by covering her face with her apron and lying face down in the dirt as the storm raged overhead. . . ."

Mama turns to Pa with worried eyes. She has barely touched the stew she has made for us.

"When do you suppose it'll hit us?"

"Sometime near dawn," he answers. He blows on the hot stew before taking a bite. I have never seen Pa get anxious or worried by news of a dust storm. This evening is no exception.

"Liam," he says, meeting my brother's eager eyes, "finish your supper, then come out and help me get the cows in the barn."

"Yes, sir!" Liam snaps. He carries his half-full bowl to the sink, slurping a spoonful as he walks.

"Now, Liam, you carry that stew back to your place and finish eating," Pa says. "You're not going to be of any use to me later tonight or tomorrow if you don't eat a good supper." Reluctantly, Liam sits back down and resumes eating, although at a faster pace than he usually would for something good as stew.

"What can I do to help?" I ask Pa, hoping he has a list of duties for me to do instead of turning me over to my mother. I'd much rather be outside making sure the animals are safe than hanging sheets over the windows and filling in the cracks in the windows with flour paste.

"You make sure the doors of the henhouse and the chicken coop are latched tight, then help your mother with the things she has to do in the house."

After dinner, we scatter off to our jobs with the seriousness of soldiers. In a way, that is what we are—soldiers—and the enemy is the oncoming storm. It is hard to believe that one is coming. The night is quiet, and a million stars are scattered across the cold, dark sky. I double-check the latches and whisper some comforting words to the chickens.

"Don't worry now," I tell them. "Pa fixed your homes tight into the ground after the last storm, so you're not gonna blow away. This storm's gonna be over before you even know it's hit."

I linger outside before going in to help Mama, taking a few more deep breaths of the clear air. If the storm is as bad as they say, we might not have clear air for nearly a week. It's the dust that hangs in the air that I hate most. You can clean away the dust that settles, but the dust in the air burns your eyes and lungs. I find the North Star, then turn to the left to face the storm blowing in from Colorado.

"You don't scare us, you black duster, you!" I yell into the night. At first it seems like a silly thing to do, but before I can stop myself, I start yelling again, bolder and louder. "You can hurt us, but you can never beat us! We're Weightmans! We're Cimarron folk, through and through!"

Chapter Sixteen
Violet

Decembertime, 1938
near Tulare, California

Dear Annie,

I've been wanting to write you a long time, but some sort of weariness has settled in me and I just couldn't write before now. There are days when my shoulders ache so much from working fields that I can't bear lifting my hands to wash my face. I'm tired all the time. One of my shoes is worn through. I keep a folded-up scrap of newspaper between my foot and the sole to keep the cold out.

If I thought about it, I'd say this weariness started working its way into me about the time we faced the Black Mountains in western Arizona. I didn't know mankind could build a road so steep. It seemed like just putting your head out the window to get a better look at the road could tip the truck over the cliff. All that climbing was awful hard on the motor. Pa fixed his eye on the temperature gauge and kept the truck at a crawl all the way up. Even so it almost overheated a dozen times or more. Ma, the twins, and I had to unload part of the car and carry some of our gear up the steepest part of the grade. The four of us walked up hairpin curves in single file, carrying the bathing tin, pots and sacks of clothes on our backs like a family of peddlers. Ma was near sick with fear of heights. She kept her eyes on her feet, watching every step she took. She couldn't bear seeing how high we were for fear she'd get too dizzy to keep going.

After all that the worst part was still ahead of us! As soon as we came down from those mountains we hit the Mojave Desert. The Mojave is a mean, ugly land bent on breaking your spirit. Imagine the dryness of Cimarron, only color it ash gray and throw together heaps of gravel to make mountains. Then make a sun so hot it burns away every living thing but cactus. You can see the heat rippling when you look off in the distance. It's like looking through a soda bottle.

I didn't believe Pa when he said we cleared the Mojave and were only a few hours away from orchards and bean fields. I made him show me exactly where we were and where the San Joaquin was on the map. The land keeps changing and changing when you travel. As soon as you get used to it looking one way, it gets different all over again.

When you first see the San Joaquin it's like looking at a picture postcard. Orchards and fields roll to the horizon like green cloth. It makes you believe every thing you ever heard about California being the land of milk and honey. But the land don't tell the truth about it here. There are all kinds of ugly things hidden in the fields, and once you know them, the San Joaquin never looks pretty again.

I'd go on to explain more what I mean, but I'm too tired to keep writing. I'm going to save up some more letters before I mail them to you. That way I only have to buy one stamp. I wish you could write me, but the way things are going, I don't know when we'll be able to settle down in one place.

I miss you.

> Your friend,
> Violet Cobble

P.S. Hard to believe we're only fifty miles from Hollywood! It seems farther away here than when we were home. That weariness has worked its way into my heart. It aches as bad as my feet. Even if I could find my way to a tap-dancing class, I don't think I'd have the spirit to dance.

Chapter Seventeen

Annie

It's funny the things that occur to you after a dust storm. Usually you're too busy during the storm to do much thinking, but afterwards the mind gets to all kinds of figuring. A day or so after a big storm, folks gather at the Golden Grain Diner to trade opinions. Some say we're heading toward the end of time. They believe God is as angry with us as He was with the folks living in Noah's time and the storms are His way of punishing us. Others joke about how they've got to clean up the dirt that blew over on them so it can blow over on someone else.

Mostly, I think about the things I know I'll never forget. It might be a story I hear or something I see or hear. I'll get a kind of sure, steady feeling, deep in my heart as if I were an old woman like Aunt Miracle, full of knowledge from living a long life, and I know that whatever it is I'm seeing and hearing, I'll remember it all my life. The way the birds always know a storm is coming, for instance. The day might be clear, the cows and the pigs might be quiet, but if suddenly the barn swallows start fluttering and squawking out of character, you know a duster is on its way. I'll never forget the sight of static electricity sparking over the roof of our truck when the storm is raging over and the air is charged with dust and wind. I'll never forget how for weeks after a big storm, we taste dust in our bread. I'll never forget the sound of the dust tapping like a million pencil points against the window. I'll never forget the stories of how people lost in the storms found their way home—a lantern hung on a porch, a wire tied from the back door to the barn, the path some-one made with his body by crawling face down from the field to the door.

My family was surprised when the storm we heard about on the radio didn't hit us by dawn. All four of us were up early to do the milking. Usually it's Liam's and my job to milk all ten of our cows before going to school. But with the storm liable to hit any time, Pa and Mama pitched in to make sure the job got done. We double-checked every lock and latch, filled in the cracks in the windows with flour-and-water paste, and wedged damp, rolled towels in the cracks around the doors. Mostly we were worried that Wisecrack would spook and kick down his stall door. He's an old horse, but still strong enough to break out of the barn if he's frightened enough. Pa nailed his door shut, then put his blinders on to help keep him calm.

Finally at mid-morning, the storm hit. We were huddled together trying to tune in the radio station in Amarillo to see how bad the storm was blowing. Years ago one of the first dust storms ruined our grandfather clock, so it's hard to know for sure how long this particular storm lasted. It wasn't a very long one, maybe only a couple of hours, but the wind was louder than in any other storm anyone in my family could remember. There were two layers of sound— the deeper sound was the wind, howling and groaning like ghosts, the higher sound was the dust, scratchy and rough like two pieces of sandpaper rubbing together.

Afterwards, before Mama let Liam and me go outside, she made us tie bandannas over our faces to keep the dust out of our mouths and lungs. As we walked, we held our hands out, watching them darken with dust still falling from the sky.

Almost all our animals survived. Six baby chicks died. Their limp, dusty bodies were pressed against the chicken wire, piled up in a corner of the coop. They were probably crowded there by the other chicks, and then suffocated as the dust blew in. Their poor little beaks hung open, and the inside of their mouths were lined with dust. Wisecrack rippled and stomped when he saw us. He reared and whinnied so much that Liam decided we shouldn't take the blinders off him just yet. "Let's give him some time to calm down," he said. The pigs grunted, begging us for slops, and the cows barely turned their heads to greet us. We buried the chicks by a fence post. I wrote out the date and R.I.P. on an old Popsicle stick, and Liam nailed it to the post. Pa asked us not to make crosses out of scraps of wood to mark the graves of our dead animals. Wood is too precious to use that way. Most times Mama has to use corncobs to light the stove. It's lucky if she has enough wood to bake a loaf of bread.

After checking on the animals, Liam ran off with Pa to see if the windmill needed repairing.

I went off to the dry lake bed. Years ago, when Pa was a boy, he used to fish for sunfish and blackies here. Now it's only an oval of land set a little lower in the earth. The only reason I or anyone else would know it was once a lake is because Pa told me so. Here is where I found my first arrowhead. Each storm seems to uncover a new layer of treasures. After a storm, I like to get here as soon as I can before the falling dust buries them again.

Today the winds have stripped the lake bed to a light, sandy soil. I'm breathing heavy under my bandanna, but I know that I probably couldn't breathe much at all if I took it off. The dust is fine as baby powder. It falls silently to the ground like a flurry of feathers. I walk to what feels like the center of the lake, then turn around slowly to scan the horizon. I can't see where the land breaks to sky. Too much dust is falling. It's too dark. If I were to keep walking this slow circle I'd lose all sense of direction. I tease myself with thoughts of being lost while the storm was blowing. "Where is my home?" I whine out loud, half laughing at myself as I pretend. "How will I ever get home?" I laugh, but then I think of Violet and her family, somewhere out west, looking for food, work, and shelter, and my game ends.

The best way to find arrowheads here in the lake bed after a storm is to take baby steps and keep your eyes on the ground. It's easy to miss one, or worse, step on one if you move too quickly. Once I broke the tip off a spearhead by a long, hard giant step. But if you move with a kind of stillness, sort of like a cougar stalking, you can find all kinds of treasures here in the lake bed. I think of it as practice for my future job as an archaeologist. One of the books I read from the library told how an archaeologist has to use tiny little picks to dig out an artifact, and soft, tiny brushes to clean it. You have to be slow and careful when you dig up the past, otherwise, you can't learn anything from what you've found.

I find six arrowheads. "One for each of the chicks that died," I think to myself as I put them in the box under my bed. It's a strange way of looking at it, I suppose. But then again, that's the sort of thing folks do in these dust days. We try to find a way of putting things in their place, try to find a way of making sense of things.

Chapter Eighteen
Violet

Januarytime, 1939
near Bakersfield

Dear Annie,

Like I was saying before, there's all kinds of ugliness and lies hidden in the fields here in California. You get told your first lie on these here handbills I write you on. Like on the back of this letter, it says, "500 workers needed for picking peaches! Good wages! Cheap lodgings!" When we got to that orchard, the foreman told us that so many hands turned up the owners had to set the wages down to one dollar a ton. Pa was so mad he almost spit in the man's face, saying it's a starving wage for a family. But Ma spoke up and said we'd take the work. When Pa calmed down he told her she said the right thing, because, after all, a few dollars is better than nothing at all. In the end, Ma, Pa, and I worked dawn to dusk for a week and made only seven dollars. Bees swarmed around us, attracted to the nectar sticking to our skin. I'd be up on a ladder or climbing branches, and they'd get stuck in my hair trying to reach my neck. We each got stung more than once. You know that fuzz on a peach? After a while it works its way into your fingertips just like cactus needles.

Mostly, I work all day alongside Ma and Pa. The twins take turns picking and watching the baby. They're too young to be working a full day. They tie Joseph under a tree so he can't crawl off. He's taking a long time to walk. I guess it's lucky, because he's easier to look after, but Ma worries that he's slow because he's not eating the right food.

Before the owners pay us our wages, they always take out a few dollars here and there. This is the other lie they hide from you when they say wages are good. They charge you for the crates and buckets and bags you use for picking. They charge you if you sleep in their tents, and they charge you for whatever you bought on credit at the camp store. The camp store is the only place you can buy food for miles around. It charges double for gas and food. Even so, it's not worth it for Ma or Pa to shop in town. By the time they'd get there, a day's wages as well as the gas would be lost. In the end we get paid almost nothing for all our hard work. Pa hasn't been able to send money to the bank back home for weeks now.

We save money by making camp along the road instead of sleeping in the farm camp. Lots of folks do this. One night a huge downpour came out of nowhere and flooded our tent. Wind tore down our tarp and uprooted trees. Trash and paper floated down the ditch, and dirty water covered me up to my shins. I thought we might all die. The baby clung around my neck. Ma and Pa carried the twins on their backs, and we scrambled up the muddy hill to the highway. The entire camp was flooded out. About forty of us huddled together on the highway, shivering together in the stormy night. Hours later folks picked us up and drove us to a church. They set us up in the basement with cots and blankets and brought us sandwiches and tea. We spent the next two nights there. Those were the most comfortable nights we've had since leaving home.

Those church folks who rescued us were nice, but mostly people in California are mean to us. They make fun of us because we're ragged and poor. They call us Okies, which is the same as calling us pigs or good-for-nothings. Lots of store windows in town have signs saying things like, "Okie money no good here" and "No Okies allowed." When we pass folks on the street, they look at us from the corner of their eyes as if we were set on stealing something. The kids are meanest of all. I heard one girl tell another that all us Okies smell. I wondered how she got that idea, because she never got close enough to know if I smell or not. After she said that, she and her friend started laughing and crossed the street to get away from us.

What bothers me most is when people say we're lazy, cheating folks who moved to California just to get on relief. I get so angry at them, I'm fit to lash out. Ma reminds me they're the ones who are ignorant. They don't know how the drought choked our land and forced us to leave home. They don't know we left friends and family behind to find honest work so we could feed ourselves and try to save our farm. I wish I could tell this to that girl who said we smell bad. If she likes the food she eats, she should like us, too.

More and more I'm realizing how strong you have to be just to keep going. At night sometimes

Chapter Nineteen

Annie

Weeks after the storm, you never know what you might find when you walk out the door in the morning. All that dust dumped on the county takes on a life of its own. One day it piles up around the house long and smooth as a huge sack of flour. The next day it disappears. Before dawn, while Mama, Liam, and I were milking the cows, Pa hitched a plow to Wisecrack to clear the county road. By early evening, it was covered up all over again. Pa doesn't mind doing this over and over again. The government pays him to keep the road clear, so for once the wind and the dust are bringing in some money rather than taking it away. This is one of the WPA jobs folks can get if they have a good horse. Wisecrack isn't the handsomest, fastest horse in Cimarron, but he's the only one for miles that hasn't died from dust pneumonia.

It's early January now, and we're making the first trip into town of the new year. At the train depot, Liam and I unload milk, cream, and butter while Pa records the load with the depot master. Our goods are shipped to Trinidad, Colorado. Truckers pick them up from there and take them all over the state. When Violet came along for the ride, she and I used to make up stories about who was using our butter on their pancakes. Liam thinks the game is too childish and won't play with me. Doesn't matter much. His imagination was never half as good as Violet's, anyway.

It's a cold, dreary day in town, like most days are now. It's only late afternoon, but already dark is coming on. Pa drops me off at the library. I'll meet up with him and Liam after I check out some books and see Mr. Coates.

The library is almost empty. The only other people there besides myself are Mr. Coates busily scribbling at his desk and an old man I believe to be one of the Barnes folks asleep in a chair. It's cold in here. Mr. Coates is wearing gloves with the fingertips cut off. He has a dark ink stain on his right middle finger that looks like it can never be washed off. It's only after I clear my throat a few times that he realizes I'm standing in front of his desk.

"Ah, Miss Weightman!" he cries, smiling as gleefully as if I've brought him a birthday cake. "How delightful to see you! How are your studies going?" Part of the fun of knowing Mr. Coates is his strange ways of phrasing things. No one else around here says things like "How delightful to see you" or calls school "your studies." I'm always tempted to ask him where he's from, but Mama says that would be rude. Besides, I think it's better keeping him a mystery. I'd prefer not to know that he's from, say, Beaver County, or Texhoma, for instance.

"School's going just fine, Mr. Coates," I answer, then go on to explain how I need to check out some books since I've gone as far as I can in the readers Miss Littlewood has.

"Excellent, my dear, excellent! The world can be a very big place for those who like to read and study. There's college, a university in New England, perhaps, maybe even foreign travel. As I recall, you want to study archaeology, is that correct?"

"Yes, sir."

"Splendid! And imagine, I am one of the first people with whom you have shared one of your finds. Only last weekend I completed that research for you with the aid of the friend I told you about. I have some rather exciting news for you." With that, Mr. Coates pulls out a manila envelope from his desk drawer. Inside is my arrowhead wrapped in tissue paper and a small white envelope addressed to me. "My friend's handwriting, I'm afraid to say, is even sloppier than my own."

January 11, 1938

Dear Miss Weightman:

Thank you for the opportunity to look at the arrowhead you found recently near your home. I must say I envy you for the rich excavating opportunities you have in your part of the county. Here in Oklahoma City it is rare to find any arrowhead, let alone one of the beauty and craftsmanship you have allowed me to look at.

Mr. Coates asked me if I thought this was made by a Comanche Indian. First of all, I must tell you I am impressed you know enough about the Plains Indians to ask such a question. When I expressed my surprise to Mr. Coates, he told me that no, not all eleven-year-olds in Cimarron know as much as you do, and that you are, in fact, quite unusual, a remarkable young lady, indeed.

And now, along with your unusual knowledge, you may add an unusual find. Your beautiful arrowhead was certainly carved by a Comanche Indian as clearly evidenced in the flaring points at the bottom of the blade where it was lashed to a wooden handle of some sort. Its length and the care with which it was carved are unusual. I doubt very much that it was used for hunting. I believe its uses were entirely ceremonial.

In fact, my own studies of the rituals and ceremonies of the Comanche lead me to believe that this was the blade of a special arrow owned by an important chief. Just as European kings commonly hold a scepter, Comanche chiefs often held a single, beautiful arrow to signify their authority. The chief held it during councils and important gatherings.

And so, Miss Weightman, I close by congratulating you on your find. Take good care of it. I hope this is the beginning of a long, interesting career in the rewarding field of archaeology.

Sincerely yours,
Professor L. Stevens
Edmond State College
Oklahoma City, Oklahoma

It's a while before I can say anything. I take the letter from Mr. Coates and read it myself. I don't dare to pick up my arrowhead yet.

"It's all very exciting, isn't it?" beams Mr. Coates. "Inevitably, the question of storing such a valuable artifact comes up. Where do you keep your collection, may I ask?"

"In an old shoe box under my bed," I answer.

"Oh, dear," says Mr. Coates shaking his head. "If you would forgive me for saying so, that will never do. No, with an arrowhead like this, you must take special care that the surface is not marred. Your other specimens will easily chip and scratch this one simply as you move the box."

"What should I do with it?"

"Something does occur to me. Often when someone owns an item of great beauty or importance, she lends it to a museum or a gallery of some sort. In exchange for the favor, the museum takes good care of the object, securing it behind a locked case for instance, making sure it will not be dropped or unduly jostled."

"But there's no museums around here," I say.

"No, but we do have a rather nice display

case with a lock near the front door of our library. It's not the British Museum, certainly, but it is a safe place. I would write out a little notecard explaining the arrowhead's importance. Underneath it I would add something like 'graciously lent to the Boise City Library by Miss Annie May Weightman.'"

I think about this silently for a few moments, then ask, "But will I ever get to touch it again? Will I ever get to look at it up close?"

"Of course, my dear! You would be the only one allowed to do so. All you have to do is ask me to unlock the case for you."

"I'm not sure about this, Mr. Coates. I need some time to think about it."

"I understand," he said nodding. "Just remember that if you decide to house it in the display case here in the library, you would be contributing to the education of everyone who saw it. The attitude of most of our neighbors toward the Indians who once lived here is rather shameful. This beautiful arrowhead of yours might help to build some knowledge and respect for those who lived here first. Perhaps we could ask Professor Stevens to loan us a few artifacts so that we can start a small museum for Cimarron County."

"Can I take this home, please?" I ask holding up the letter. I'm thinking about a museum right here in Cimarron, one I can help start.

"Of course. It is your letter. And the arrowhead?" I pause for a moment, not sure quite what to say. I feel torn between wanting to take it home and wanting to keep it safe.

"Why don't you keep it in your desk for now," I answer.

"Certainly. I'll take very good care of it. I lock my desk every evening before going home. Good-bye, Miss Weightman."

"Good-bye, Mr. Coates."

By the time we get home, it's completely dark outside. Mama has set the table and hurries us to wash up for supper. I can tell that she's a little irritated that we were gone so long, and I wasn't at home helping her. After supper there are still the dishes to be done and the cows to be milked. Before too long, she'll be asking me to stay home instead of going into town with Pa and Liam. As we get older, Liam is taking on certain chores and I'm taking on others. Liam is doing more outside chores like repairing the fence and going to the depot with

Pa, and I'm doing more inside ones like bleaching the sheets and baking the bread. I can't say I like this much, but I suppose I'm luckier than some girls. If Mama had more babies, I might even have to quit school.

Because of her mood, I'm a little shy to tell her the news about my arrowhead. It's Pa who brings it up at the dinner table. Mama watches him as he talks. When he's finished, she smiles at me, but says nothing. Liam is happy to repeat the advice he gave me when he first heard the story on the drive home.

"Mr. Coates is making you a good deal, Annie," he says. "You should let him put that arrowhead in the display case where it will be safe."

"Besides that, Annie, you might get famous," Pa chuckles. "Just imagine, 'graciously lent to this library by Miss Annie May Weightman.'"

"Just don't let it swell that head of yours," says Mama. She smiles when she says it, but it spoils my appetite some. I stir my bowl of pork and beans watching the steam disappear into thin air.

Chapter Twenty
Violet

Marchtime, 1939

Dear Annie,

What I've learned most about hard times, is that, if you let them, they can turn you cold and silent like a field of stones. Being hungry and tired, being cheated out of wages and called dirty names robs you body and soul. These things can break your spirit. I've been watching the worry lines on my Ma's face get more and more set, as if they were carved into her forehead.

I've been trying to figure out ways to keep going. At night, I tell the twins stories I remember from the books I used to read to Aunt Miracle. About the time I wrote you my last letter, I realized I needed something more for myself, something secret connecting me with home. I feel shy telling you what I've been doing with the corn dolls we played with when we were small.

I never told you, but I went on dressing and

talking to my dolls, clear up to the time Aunt Miracle died. After that, it really did feel like I was too old to play with them. Still, I took them when we left home. I held them on my lap as we drove west looking for work. Sometimes I even brought them with me into the fields, hiding them under the bib of my overalls. I'd pretend one was you and another was Aunt Miracle, and I'd talk to them as I worked the orchards and the fields.

Late one night, a hoot owl woke me up. I couldn't get back to sleep. I tossed and turned, listening to my family breathing in the dark. Finally, without really knowing what I was going to do, I took my dolls from underneath my pillow of bundled-up rags and left our tent. I walked a ways outside of camp and sat by a creek under a willow tree. Without thinking much about it, I pulled out one of the kernels still there under the papa doll's hat and planted it. I sat there in the night, imagining a path of corn leading me back home. Ever since then, I've been planting a kernel at every place we camp. Somehow it comforts me as we head out on the road again, not knowing where we'll be staying and how long we'll be there.

I've been afraid to tell you, fearing you'd say it is an awful silly thing to do. But then I got to *thinking about it. In a way I think it's a lot like what you're doing when you go looking for arrowheads. We're both putting our hands and minds to the earth, discovering stories and searching for who we are. You used to say we're so different. I'm more airy, you're more down to earth. I don't think it's true anymore. It's taken me all these miles to see how alike we really are. We were born to a barren, dusty land. Folks say it can't grow nothing, but it grew us spirited and mindfull. We know beneath the broken land there's treasures in the dust.*

When I finish this, I'll plant another seed. I'll think of its roots reaching out to those of all the other seeds I've planted. In my mind I'll conjure up the road I'm growing at my back, the green path leading back to Aunt Miracle and home and you.

Love from your friend,
Violet Cobble

Chapter Twenty-One
Annie

Ever since we talked about what to do with my arrowhead, Mr. Coates and I have been turning a corner of the library into the Cimarron County Museum. He asked me if I would like to help him, and, of course, I agreed. I go in Saturday mornings and help him catalogue and organize some of the artifacts we're going to display. Folks from all over the county have been donating things to start up our museum. At first I objected to showing things like old Mr. Shelter's glass eye, a two-headed calf's skull, and a nine-foot-long diamondback skin complete with rattler.

"These aren't really scientific," I complained. "They're more like things you'd find in some kind of freak show. These things aren't gonna teach anybody anything."

"I agree with you, Annie. But unfortunately, many of our neighbors have little imagination or any desire to learn. Curiosity is something they do possess, however, and objects like these will bring them in to our museum. Scientific, no. Yet these objects serve a valuable purpose. Perhaps they will trick some of our neighbors into learning."

"Hmmm," I respond. It's irritating to think we're working so hard just to trick people. "I guess it's what being a teacher is like."

"Oh, yes!" Mr. Coates beams. His hair needs combing. It looks like he has owl wings attached to the sides of his head. "I have always felt that one of the most important goals of teachers, librarians, and museums is to trick the reluctant into learning."

Pa has been encouraging me to help start the museum. He lets me ride Wisecrack on the Saturdays he doesn't drive into town himself. He even built two display cabinets out of materials Mr. Coates got the general store to donate. He stained and sanded them real nice and added a little brass padlock on the front.

Mama, on the other hand, makes me feel like I'm sneaking out of chores. She still cooks me breakfast and packs me a lunch, but she acts awful tired and forlorn, sighing often and moving slow. She never asks questions about how we're getting on or what we're going to exhibit in the museum. Instead, she gives orders.

"See that you're home by early afternoon," she says, her mouth a thin, straight line. "And don't run poor old Wisecrack just so you can get back in time to milk the cows."

It's Saturday morning and my breath makes little white clouds in the cold air. I'm banging my lunch pail, an old syrup bucket, against my thigh, hoping Pa will hurry up and get the truck going. I'm wondering if Mama is mad enough that she didn't pack me a good lunch. I pry the lid open with my pocketknife. A cheese sandwich and a tin of beans. Same as usual. She can't be too angry. Even so, I'm feeling so guilty and angry that I mention it to Pa when we're driving into town.

"She doesn't want me helping Mr. Coates, Pa. She doesn't act at all interested in what I'm doing. She'd rather have me stay home and help her do the laundry."

"Well, I'm not sure that's exactly what your mother wants. It's a little more complicated than that. The way I see it, you're on some kind of path. It's the same one you've been on ever since you started reading and getting interested in arrowheads and archaeology. Only now it's more clear to your mother and me. We talk about it sometimes. We both think it's good, and we're proud of you. Only thing is, I see it as a path that's taking you somewhere. And your mother sees it as a path that's taking you away."

"But I don't want to go away, Pa," I look out the window, knowing I'm not telling the truth. Rising dust makes a smoky trail behind us. It hangs in the air awhile before drifting down to cover the bramble. "I mean, maybe when I'm older and digging up caveman things or excavating some ancient city. But that's not for a long time. I've got to get through school before anything like that happens."

"Oh, honey," Pa laughs. "That's not far away. Your mama knows you're thinking like this, that's why she's having a hard time with you helping Mr. Coates. See, folks in Cimarron never left before the drought came. Folks stayed in one place, married their neighbors, raised their kids, and stayed around to work their daddy's farm and take care of their folks when they got old. Most mothers never had a daughter like you, one who was raring to go off and study things."

"Still seems a long way off to me," I said, feeling glum. We're close to town now. I can see the grain towers by the depot. They've been empty for years.

"Of course it does, Annie. Time passes slow when you're a child. But you'll see. One day soon, this drought will be over. Next thing you know you'll be grown up."

"This drought's never gonna be over." We turn onto Main Street. Pa waves to a few men in overalls talking outside the cafe.

"Oh, it will. It rained last week in Elkhart. Didn't last more than a few minutes, but it was rain just the same. I think it means we're in for a wet spring."

"Really, Pa?"

"It's only a hunch. But I'm not the only one who's hopeful. We'll see."

Mr. Coates is glad to see us. He shakes hands with Pa, thanking him again for the display cases and telling him what a good worker I am.

"I've got some business to take care of. I'll be back in a couple of hours." Pa waves good-bye, then heads out the door to the general store.

I set up working at Mr. Coates's desk. Today I'm writing descriptions and acknowledgments on little pale-yellow cards. Mr. Coates has given me a list to work from. I dip my pen in the pot of ink and write, "Three-legged chicken, generously donated by Mr. Elmore Creed of Boise City." I sigh. Mr. Coates looks up. He is sitting on the floor. Tattered baskets, bones, and arrowheads are spread around him in a semi-circle.

"Have I given you a tedious job, Annie?"

"To be honest, sir, it's not very exciting."

"Perhaps this will be more to your liking." Gently, he places the arrowheads in a bucket, then gives it to me. "We need to wash the dirt and mud off these artifacts. Here's an old toothbrush and a few rags. Go round back and use the pump. Remember! Be gentle!"

Outside it's cold. I button my jacket all the way, then fill the pail just enough so the arrowheads are covered. I slowly rake my fingers through the cloudy water and rub away the dirt with my fingertips. The only sound to be heard is the arrowheads grating against the tin pail. My fingers get a little achy from the cold, but I keep working the mud away. Some of it is so old and tough it's like gritty cement. Working your hands on the past this way, trying to break it free so it can speak, sets your mind to thinking. Maybe Pa's right and the drought will be over soon. Maybe the earth's orbit is bringing our county into some kinder relation to the sun. Maybe Violet will come back and we'll grow up together, each loving our own things but being together again. I bet the Indian who carved this arrowhead was thinking something like this as he was chipping stone with stone. I bet he was watching his hands at work, thinking about his loved ones and wondering what the future might bring.

Chapter Twenty-Two
Violet

Apriltime, 1939
Weedpatch Camp,
near Bakersfield, California

Dear Annie,

Everytime I think I see something terrible, another thing comes along that makes my heart even sicker. We were heading out of the Faber Ranch, where we were picking oranges. There was a big harvest, so the farmers hired a field full of workers but only paid us 20 cents an hour. In the end we didn't make enough to buy beans or meat at the store. For three days all we ate was fried dough. Ma and I made little patties of flour, water, and lard and fried them up in bacon grease. Fried dough tastes miserable. It lies heavy in your stomach. Even if there was plenty of it to eat, it won't make you feel satisfied. There ain't enough taste in it.

After we ate supper, we headed out with the

rest of the hands. There was a long line of trucks, all of us waiting to check out and collect our money. All of a sudden, a few cars ahead of us, there was some kind of commotion. Some men were yelling and running off in the distance, leaving their trucks with the engine going. Guards with rifles charged them. They pointed their guns at them yelling, "Don't make any trouble!" and "Get back to your trucks." We looked to see what the men were running toward and what the guards were protecting. We didn't see nothing at first, but then one of the twins pointed out the window, yelling, "There's a fire over yonder!" As soon as he said it, I could smell it in the air— a sweet, burning smell. The farmers were setting a great big pile of oranges on fire. The pile was tall as Pa, and big as four or five trucks pulled together. We couldn't believe what we were seeing. Pa leaned his head out the window and asked the driver behind us what in heck they were doing. The man said the farmers were doing this in order to keep prices high. He said if there's too many oranges for sale, the price drops and the farmer loses his profit. Ma started crying when she heard this. "My baby's not walking cause he ain't eating right, and those farmers are burning

Then, he got his left arm crippled. He said it was nearly torn off in a threshing machine. Most farmers won't hire him 'cause they say he can't work fast enough. All he wants is to go back to Oklahoma and live with his brother's family, but he needs money for the road and then some more to bring home so he won't be a burden to his family. Pa said money was hard to come by. Mr. Shyrock said he has a plan, but he needs another man to help him. He wants to sneak aboard a freight car into Los Angeles and find work in the city. He says there's all kinds of day jobs at the depot or the port, maybe even pumping gas at a gas station. "Why don't you go ahead and do it yourself?" Pa asked, but Mr. Shyrock shook his head. He says it's too dangerous for a one-armed man to ride the rails alone. He needs someone to help him get on board, and then help him defend himself if it came down to that.

Pa told him our situation, how we're trying to get enough money so the bank won't take our farm and then go back home. He said he ain't seen nothing in California to make him want to stay. Folks are mean and money hungry and surviving is just as hard here as it is back home. "Looks like we both aim to get back to

Oklahoma," said Mr. Shyrock. "Ain't many of us longing for that dusty land, but here we are, Arthur."

Turns out, Pa and Mr. Shyrock headed out together to try their luck riding the rails and finding work in Los Angeles. It gave me a worried, lonely feeling saying good-bye to Pa. He might be gone for weeks before we see him, and until then Ma and I are alone here in the Weedpatch Camp with Joseph and the twins. At least it's clean here. Ma and I are cleaning the bathrooms to pay our rent for our tent, and we've got enough money for all of us to have breakfast every morning. Mr. Shyrock left us a bag of beans and some salt pork. He said he and Pa couldn't cook it up anyway. Other folks have been nice to us, sharing what food they can. We do our best to make it up to them by helping out with their washing and cleaning.

So for now, we're staying at the Weedpatch Camp, waiting for Pa. In a couple of weeks or so there should be field work nearby, planting broccoli or lettuce. If Pa is still gone, the twins and I will go look for work with some other family while Ma stays here with the baby.

I will send you all the letters I've written,

since we might be here awhile. When you get them, I hope you will write me back. Folks can get letters here because it is run by the federal government. It's called the Weedpatch Camp and it's near Bakersfield, California.

Love from Violet

Chapter Twenty-Three

Annie

May 13, 1939
Cimarron County, Oklahoma

Dear Violet,

After supper this evening, Mama told me I didn't have to help her wash the dishes. She said I might like to spend my time reading something special, and then she handed me an envelope full of letters from you. I have read all of your letters many times over. When I fold them up, I make sure I follow the crease lines and fold them the same way you did.

I let Pa and Mama read your letters, and we're all sorry you and your folks have had such a hard time since leaving Oklahoma. We're hoping Mr. Shyrock and your pa find some good day jobs in Los Angeles so you can come back home. Even if they don't, you should come back home anyway. Every few days or so it rains a little, and if it keeps up, Pa says he's going to buy some seed and plant summer wheat in the field near the lake bed. Pa says he could sure use your Pa's help tilling the field. It's tough as concrete from all these dry years. If he brings in a crop, he says he'll share part of the profit with your family to help get you started back here at home.

Pa was talking about planting wheat with some old timers at the general store in Boise City last Saturday. Some of them said he's foolish, because there hasn't been enough rain. But Pa is still planning on it. He thinks there's been enough to make the grasses come back, and if they do, he'll plant his wheat field. I've been watching the ground for little shoots of grass. Mama says they'll be greenish-yellow at first, and then, if the rain is steady and the roots hold, they'll turn dark green.

When you are home, I'll show you the museum Mr. Coates and I have set up in the library. I'm exhibiting the arrowhead I found when we were hunting for weeds for the cows. It is a real Comanche arrowhead. A friend of Mr. Coates says it probably belonged to the chief and was used in ceremonies.

I miss you.

Love,
Annie

Chapter Twenty-Four
Violet

Junetime, 1939
Rte. 66, near Wikieup, Arizona

Dear Annie,

We were packing our gear, getting ready to head out of Weedpatch Camp, when the camp manager ran up to us. "I wouldn't want Violet to miss this," he said and handed me your letter. It felt like I had been handed something magic, like that sword King Arthur got from the fairies. I'm carrying it next to my corn dolls in my overalls pocket close to my heart. Just think—if Pa and Mr. Shyrock hadn't had such a hard time getting the motor going I wouldn't have never seen it.

We were all real happy to hear about the rain coming back to the panhandle. We've heard folks talk about it at Weedpatch, but when you hear it from one of your own neighbors in a letter you receive yourself, it seems more likely. Pa and Mr. Shyrock have been talking about planting wheat ever since I read your letter to them.

Pa and Mr. Shyrock were gone six weeks or more. It took them three days of hopping boxcars to get to a busy depot outside Los Angeles. Folks were glad to have them there to help unload cattle cars since they were both raised working cattle and dairy cows. They drove them onto trucks and hitched rides with the drivers to the slaughterhouse where they worked for a nice long spell making good money, the best money they've made since leaving home. Mr. Shyrock says the manager at the slaughterhouse hired him right away. There are plenty of things a strong, one-armed man can do in a slaughterhouse, and he was glad to meet someone who would give him a chance to work. He said if he wasn't yearning to get home he might have stayed there. Pa agreed. He says it sure beat picking peaches, but that he could never trade Oklahoma for a life in California slaughtering cattle, especially now that the rains might be returning.

We still need to make all the money we can so we can pay off our debt and get us on our feet once we're home. We've been working the fields in Wikieup picking carrots and lettuce.

Like I said, your letter came just as we were

ready to leave Weedpatch Camp. After I read it, I took my corncob dolls and walked to the edge of camp. I dug out the last few kernels and planted them under a willow tree. Now there's none left. I'm on my way home with my path of corn growing at my back.

Love from your friend,
Violet Cobble

Chapter Twenty-Five

Annie

Now that I know Violet is on her way home, Liam and I visit the Cobble house more often. Those two wild cats still live under the porch. They run out to see us when they hear our steps, meowing for the scraps of ham we bring them. Liam says we'll tame them if we feed them regularly. Then they'll be less likely to run off once the Cobbles take over their place again. Pa comes with us every now and then to clear the weeds and brambles growing around their house.

Even though she's back on the road, I've been writing Violet and sliding the letters under her front door. They're not very interesting letters, more like a diary really, but at least she'll know how I've been thinking of her. I told her about setting up the museum and the little party we had the day it opened to the public. In general, folks are most interested in the glass eye and the two-headed calf skull. Every now and then, someone takes an interest in the arrowhead collection, so Mr. Coates says we should feel proud. I let Violet know how Thelma Schiller is coming along with her reading and how her pa, rumored to be the meanest man in the county, came over to my mother at the museum party to tell her how thankful he is that I'm helping Thelma. Sometimes I write about the facts I'm learning in the books Mr. Coates picks out for me to read—facts about Ice Age Man building his home from mammoth bones and stretching bison hides over them so he can keep warm.

There's a knothole in a piece of lumber Mr. Cobble nailed over one of the front windows of his place. If I stand on my tiptoes, I can look into the empty house. A thin layer of dust covers the bare floor, collecting in a small drift on the opposite wall. Near the middle of the room are a broken cup and a worn shoe. It's a child's shoe, probably one that belonged to Violet before it was passed on to one of the twins. A tattered curtain stretches across the doorway to the kitchen. A picture of Jesus holding a baby lamb hangs crookedly above it.

Sometimes as I peer into Violet's empty house, my mind runs through memories. I'll see us reading to Aunt Miracle while the twins build a town out of matchboxes. I'll see us playing with our corncob dolls or dressing up in old sheets and acting out a fairy tale, she being the fairy godmother and the princess and the prince, me being a tree in the forest or a footman at the ball.

I think about what I would say if I were an archaeologist who came upon this house out of the blue and had to study it. I guess I would say that the people who once lived here were good folks, modest folks, who had to leave in a hurry. They were facing some kind of hardship that made it so they had to pick up and go quick. It seems like they were hoping to come back because they took the time to protect their windows. There really aren't enough clues to finish the story. Only Violet can do that. Only she can say what she lost and found by leaving and coming back.

How far can the roots of a cornstalk reach? I like pretending they can reach a thousand miles. Any day now, when I'm sitting on the earth digging for arrowheads, I know my hand will touch a web of thin white roots, Violet's roots reaching back home.

Chapter Twenty-Six
Violet

Annie says I've gotten scrunched up since I've been away. It's the first thing she says to me.

"You used to be taller than me," she frowns. "Let's stand back-to-back."

We're on my front porch. Our mothers' happy voices drift through the open windows like thistledown. They're cleaning cobwebs in the kitchen and washing down the pantry shelves. Mrs. Weightman has brought a cake over, and the twins are eating it with their bare hands, smearing frosting all over their faces. Baby Joseph is holding on to the table leg, trying to stand.

Annie runs her hand over our two heads, checking our height.

"Stand up straighter!" she orders.

My chest grows big and free as I lift my chin and take a deep breath. All of a sudden, it feels like my heart is filling with warm water. My eyes grow wide to take in the view in front of me. Our yard is covered with weeds and young grass. They're fragile and yellow, and I know if I see one shoot bend too sharply or break in the wind, I'll start to cry. I'm full of hope for myself and my family, so I don't dare let a tear fall for fear I'll jinx us. I bite my lip to stop myself from crying.

"Well, I'm taller now," says Annie. She takes me around back to show me where two cats live under our house.

"They used to be wild as bobcats, but Liam and I tamed them for you. They're probably watching us. If you creep up meowing and act like you're holding some food, they'll come out."

Annie and I kneel down, holding out our hands, meowing and singing, "Here kitty-kitty-kitty. Here kitty-kitty-kitty." Part of me thinks it's mean promising food when there isn't any, but I don't say anything to Annie. Things don't seem real to me yet.

Two sleek gray cats slink out into the sunlight. They bat their eyes a bit and sniff delicately at our outstretched hands. If it weren't for the different patches of white, they could be twins. One has white paws. The other has a streak on her chest stretching all the way to her belly. When they've made up their minds we don't have any food, their tails twitch and snap with anger. The one with the white paws cuffs my hand, but her claws aren't extended. They both dart off, their tails swishing through the tall weeds.

"It's gonna take a while for them to get to know you," says Annie.

"I'll wait," I answer. "I ain't going nowhere."

ABOUT THE AUTHOR

Tracey Porter teaches English at a middle school in Santa Monica, California. A poet whose work has appeared in various magazines and anthologies, she is a graduate of Georgetown University and the University of London, England. Of her inspiration to write about Oklahoma during the Great Depression, Ms. Porter says, "I remember the very day, where I was sitting, what the weather was like outside the classroom, when I first saw images from and learned about the Dust Bowl in my eighth-grade U.S. history class." Greatly influenced by Dorothea Lange's and Arthur Rothstein's photographs of Okies, and by John Steinbeck's GRAPES OF WRATH, Ms. Porter traveled to Cimarron County, Oklahoma, to complete her research for TREASURES IN THE DUST, her first novel. She lives in Los Angeles with her husband, Sandy, daughter, Sarah, and son, Sam.

Good book –
easy reading –
Dust Bowl